To John Ray Jeppson

Norby and the Court Jester

NORBY AND THE COURT JESTER

Janet and Isaac Asimov

Walker and Company
New York

First published in the United States of America in 1991 by Walker Publishing Company, Inc.

Published simultaneously in Canada by Thomas Allen & Son Canada, Limited, Markham, Ontario

Library of Congress Cataloging-in-Publication Data
Asimov, Janet.
Norby and the court jester / by Janet and Isaac Asimov.
p. cm.
Summary: While visiting the toy and game fair on planet Izz, Jeff and Norby search for a missing robot and the villain responsible for sabotaging the planet's computer system.
ISBN 0-8027-8131-4. —ISBN 0-8027-8132-2 (lib. bdg.)
[1. Robots—Fiction. 2. Science fiction. 3. Mystery and detective stories.] I. Asimov, Isaac, 1920– . II. Title.
PZ7.A836Nh 1991
[Fic]—dc20 91-18432
CIP
AC

Printed in the United States of America

2 4 6 8 10 9 7 5 3 1

Contents

Norby and the Court Jester

1.

Spring Vacation

"Norby! What have you done to my computer terminal?"

"I'm only trying to help, Jeff. I just inserted a program that will help you learn Unified Field Theory for the second exam. If you'd paid attention to my teaching, you wouldn't have failed the first exam and delayed our departure for Izz."

Cadet Jefferson Wells glared at the one and only mixed-up robot in the Terran Federation, or anywhere else as far as he knew. Norby looked virtuously shiny today, having polished the silvery metal of his barrel body and the wide-brimmed, domed metal hat on his half of a head. Norby stood on his extensible legs in front of his own computer terminal in their room at Space Academy, playing Jeff's favorite computer game with his back eyes closed in concentration.

It was not possible to tell at a glance that Norby was indeed a robotic mixture, put together by an old spacer out of Terran and alien mechanisms, or that he had special talents like being able to travel through hyperspace to faraway planets only a few people in the Federation knew existed.

"These math riddles you programmed are going to take forever, Norby. Rinda will be annoyed."

"I'm sure the crown princess of Izz will understand. Too bad the Izzian computer system isn't compatible with ours. I suppose I *could* rig up something for you."

Jeff gritted his teeth. "I am going to Izz, and I'm not going to study Unified Field Theory or have anything to do with computer programs while I'm there. Just because I flunked one little exam doesn't mean I can't enjoy myself."

1

One of Norby's back eyelids shot up. "If you'll turn around and look at your monitor, you'll see that Admiral Yobo's personal seal has shoved the equations out. Better answer."

"What have I done now!" Jeff gulped and touched a switch. To his surprise, Boris Yobo's majestic head did not replace the Yobo coat of arms on the monitor, but the admiral's bass voice filled the room.

"Cadet Wells! Your brother has informed me that you're going to spend your spring vacation in a certain exceedingly distant pleasure spot. I have decided to join you. We can make the trip in my private minicruiser. What is the, ah, Izzian occasion?"

"It's their annual toy and game fair, sir. I thought it would be relaxing to play games after studying."

"It has come to my attention that you have not been studying enough, Cadet. You flunked Unified Field Theory."

"Are you commanding Norby and me to stay here for vacation?" asked Jeff as Norby winked at him. The admiral could not travel to Izz without Norby, for the Federation had not yet replaced its one hyperdrive ship, stolen and wrecked by the exiled villain Ing the Ingrate.

"You'll have to study on Izz, young man. I do not intend to vacation anywhere in the Federation, because people keep calling me to argue about the proposed Space Command pension plans. Since I have abolished compulsory retirement and expect to die in harness, the plans do not interest me. I want a vacation free of verbal battles, disgruntled underlings, bollixed-up computer systems— By the way, did Norby have anything to do with the fact that Field Theory math has infiltrated the order-of-duty schedules and no one knows when to go on duty?"

"Perhaps people in Space Command should brush up on their math," Norby said.

There was an ominous silence for a moment, and then Yobo said, in a deeper bass, "I see. All too well. Cadet, I think it will be best if you take your impossible robot away from Space Command for a few days so my computer technicians can straighten things out unencumbered. Meet me at my ship in an hour. We will go immediately to Izz. Toys and games, eh?"

The Admiral's seal winked out of the holovision monitor. Jeff sighed and opened his already packed suitcase. "I'll bring the textbook I printed out. I wish I could take one of the computer instruction programs. And blast, I forgot. I'll have to put braids in my hair."

"I'll do it for you, Jeff. Good thing you haven't had your hair cut for a while. It's long enough to braid into a little pigtail."

Jeff ran his fingers through his curly brown hair and groaned. It was absolutely essential to have at least some portion of one's hair braided while on Izz. Only the royal family was allowed to go without braids.

As Norby's two-way hands grabbed Jeff's back hair, the pain reminded Jeff that he'd also forgotten to tell Admiral Yobo to buy a braided wig. When a strange alien species called the Others took paleolithic humans from all over Earth to settle them on the terraformed planet Izz, they somehow got a sample of humanity that did not possess any genes for baldness.

Admiral Yobo always said that with a perfectly shaped head hair was unnecessary, but the fact remained. He was *bald*.

In the control room of Yobo's minicruiser, *The Pride of Mars*, Jeff and Norby waited. And waited. Jeff loosened the pigtail that Norby had made too tight and worried about the repeat exam he'd have to take as soon as he returned to Space Academy. Norby fiddled with the ship's computer until he got a reasonable semblance of the game Minimicro going.

"I should improve this game, Jeff. Turn it into a feely."

"Feelies are for pretending you're right in a battle with the villain you've chosen, or courting the prettiest girl. You can't make a feely to let the player know what it's like to mess around with molecules."

"I had in mind experiencing life on the subatomic level."

"There is no life there. Life is molecules and up."

"Jeff, don't you ever learn anything? Molecules are composed of atoms, and atoms are made of subatomic particles, which are made of gluons, quarks, and leptons, which are aspects of the field . . ."

"Stop, Norby. A quark can't feel anything. What's the point of making a feely game about things that small?"

Norby blinked. "It appeals to my emotive circuits. I'd like to experience things on that small a level, except that down there things are just probabilities. But you're right, Jeff. It would be hard to have an interesting game, unless we stuck in some surprises. Like telepathy. I've always thought my telepathic powers operate through probability fields . . ."

"Which explains why they're so erratic."

The door to the control room slid open and Boris Yobo entered, resplendent in his favorite African tunic over trousers that were full, if not quite as baggy as the regulation costume on Izz. His black head shone as if Norby had polished it, too, and his dark eyes beamed.

"Admiral!" shouted Norby. "There's a huge insect attacking your face! Don't move—I'll save you . . ."

Yobo raised a large palm toward Norby. "Robot, if you touch my moustache, I'll have your insides removed so the queen of Izz can use your barrel for storing plurf."

"Sir," Jeff said cautiously, after managing to gaze with a straight face at Yobo's latest acquisition, "how did you get those tiny braids in your moustache?"

"The braids are why I'm late. Remembering the peculiar laws of Izz, I decided to braid my new moustache, but neither I nor the service's barber could manage it. The head surgeon, with tweezers, a mini-hemostat, and a judicious amount of gel, succeeded."

4

"How did you explain why you wanted them?"

"I told him I was going to a fancy-dress ball. He had the nerve to laugh, saying I could stand at the entrance to keep out the riff and the raff. Doctors never have the proper respect for authority." Yobo peered at Jeff. "What's the matter, Cadet? Do you disapprove of my moustache?"

"Oh, no, sir. You look almost—well, very . . ."

"Piratical," Norby said. "A peculiar pirate. Better shave it off and buy a braided wig."

"Wigs are much too hot," said Yobo, seating himself in one of the chairs and yawning. "Norby, get in the control chair, hook up your hyperdrive, and take us to Izz."

"Yes, s— Hey!"

"What now?" Yobo sat up. "Cadet, has your robot deactivated or merely gone into a trance?"

Norby's lid of a hat had slammed down onto his body so that his eyes were no longer visible. His sensor wire extruded full length from the knob on his hat and seemed to quiver.

"He's listening."

"To what? We haven't turned the motor on yet."

"Perhaps to a telepathic message. I hope nothing bad."

Norby's hat shot up, the wire withdrew, and his hands went to the ship's computer console. Instantly, the ship's engine revved up, there was a lurch, and the viewscreen filled with the empty grayness of hyperspace.

"What's the hurry, Norby?" asked Jeff while Yobo muttered about robots who didn't know how to handle delicate machinery like the engine of his beloved *Pride*.

"Pera sent a telepathic message."

"I thought she wasn't very good at telepathy." Rinda's little robot, Pera, had been made by the Others as a Perceiver, someone to observe and record phenomena. She did not have Norby's hyperdrive ability and was only slightly telepathic.

5

"She isn't. That's why I'm not sure what she was saying, but I do know that part of it was the word 'help.' "

"Help for herself or for someone else?" asked Yobo.

"I don't know. Another word I caught was 'Ing.' "

Yobo grimaced. "I have always regretted letting Rinda take Ing back to Izz as court jester. He should have been brought back to the Federation to be tried as a traitor."

"We couldn't do that, sir," said Jeff. "He'd have told everyone about Norby's talents, and the existence of Izz."

"True, Cadet, but if Ing is messing up Izz, I'll deal with him. He's a scoundrel."

"Maybe Pera needs help *for* Ing."

"We'll soon know," said Norby. "There's Izz."

The ship had come out of hyperspace right on target. Jeff looked down on the beautiful ocean of Izz, which contained only one major continent and a southern semicircle of islands all the same size except for one large island in the middle of the chain.

"Good-looking planet," said Yobo. "Almost the equal of Earth. Nice that the Others took vegetation as well as animals from Earth when they terraformed it. Are you able to reach Pera better now?"

"No." Norby blinked several times, showing that his emotive circuits were agitated. "I can't make any contact with her even though I'm in orbit. We'd better get down to the palace at once and notify the queen."

"But Norby—the traffic patterns . . ." Jeff's warning was ignored as the *Pride* hurtled downward through the atmosphere, aimed at the main city on the continent. Izzcapital glittered, for it was literally paved with gold, a common metal on Izz.

"Cadet, what's a toy fair? It's not something I've had time to investigate in my years at Space Command."

"We have them on Earth, Admiral. Toy and game manufacturers demonstrate samples of their wares to toy buyers. I gather that on Izz the public is allowed in."

6

Yobo grunted and then said, "Norby! How can you navigate with both front eyes closed? Is the ship on autopilot?"

"I'm concentrating, trying to reach Pera—oops!"

The *Pride*, weaving through the traffic patterns over Izzcapital, crunched into the nether end of a slowly moving airtruck, whose cargo hatch slid open, producing a sudden rain of Izzian vegetables. The robotized truck stopped to hover on antigrav over its fallen cargo, which now littered the palace front steps.

A female voice yelled through the ship's loudspeakers in official-sounding Izzian. "Unregistered space vessel! This is the police. Descend to receive your traffic violation. Do not delay. Descend at once!"

2.

Officer Luka and Friend

"A formidable voice," Yobo said meditatively. "But not quite as formidable as the queen's. I hope."

Jeff nodded. "It sounds like Officer Luka, who tried to arrest us the first time we came to Izz."

Norby landed the ship in the broad open space before the vegetable-decorated palace steps, next to a small silver-striped police vehicle. "She is indeed Officer Luka," he said, "looking annoyed."

She strode from her airlock, leaving it open behind her, and pointed a stun weapon at the *Pride*. "Come out! You are all under arrest!"

Yobo muttered, "Why is it when I travel with Norby I always seem to get into trouble?" He led the way through the *Pride's* airlock, his moustache bristling.

Jeff looked up at the glittering spires of Izzpalace and thought he saw someone waving from a high window in a far tower. Trying to figure out who it could be, he tripped over a cabbage and was now looking straight at Luka's shiny boots.

Someone nearby laughed, but when Jeff realized it wasn't Luka, he glimpsed a dark figure standing in the shadow just inside the patrol ship's airlock. A few passersby observed the arrest from a distance, but on the whole the main city square of Izzcapital was remarkably empty of people.

Luka's pigtails seemed longer, her gold helmet fancier, and she had more silver braid on her stiff tunic. Jeff thought that for some reason she looked prettier.

"Hello, Officer Luka," Jeff said as he got to his feet. "Don't

8

you remember us, from the Terran Federation? I'm Jeff Wells, this is Admiral Yobo, and my robot, Norby."

"Who was driving?"

"I was," said Norby, "but I was worried about . . ."

"You are a very poor space-vehicle driver, dumping vegetables in front of the palace. Why have you come to Izz?"

"We hoped to be able to spend our vacation on Izz, attending the Royal Toy and Game Fair," Yobo said.

"And we've come to see our friend the Crown Princess Rinda." Jeff emphasized the "our friend" to impress Luka.

Luka waved the stun gun at Jeff. "That is a lie, for the crown princess is ill and cannot see anyone. If you are her friends you would not be ignorant of these facts."

"We've been away," said Jeff.

"Far, far away," added Norby.

Luka lifted a shapely eyebrow. "I have never understood exactly where your Terran Federation is located, but surely you are within reach of Izzian holov, which announced the illness of the crown princess."

"We didn't hear it," said Yobo. "What illness?"

"Ickyspot." It sounded even worse in Izzian. "She has a mild case, but since it is highly contagious she must be in quarantine like any other patient." Luka tapped the gun with her fingers. "Now about this traffic accident . . ."

"The airtruck sustained no structural damage." Norby pointed upward. "The collision sprung the hatch open, no doubt due to faulty design. It was our own ship that got dented, so we ought to sue . . ."

"My *Pride!*" Yobo examined the small dent in her nose. "Yes, I'll definitely sue." He scowled at Norby. "Somebody."

"The fault is yours," Luka insisted. She pointed to the piles of vegetables, most of them the hard, lumpy root kind. "In addition to the fine the queen will undoubtedly impose on all of you, as chief of police in Izzcapital I am informing you that if every one of those food items is not put back in the airtruck at once, you will all be dunked in the Pool of Plurf and exiled from the city."

"Why can't the airtruck pick up its own cargo?" asked Jeff. "They do on Earth."

"Izzian trucks are loaded and unloaded by robots. Traffic accidents are not anticipated, for Izzians obey the laws. Now pick up those vegetables immediately."

"Tell me, Officer," Yobo said in his friendliest voice, "just what is plurf?"

"A chemical designed to adhere to human skin. Once there, and only there, it begins to give off a peculiarly penetrating odor that does not wash away. It wears off in about a month."

"Then plurf doesn't affect robots," Norby said cheerfully.

"It has been known to deactivate robots."

"Oh . . . Admiral, Jeff, if you pick up the veggies, I'll carry them up to the truck."

Groaning, Admiral Yobo bent down and started the job. Jeff followed, trying to pick up as many as he could as quickly as possible so the admiral wouldn't get a stiff back. But the job was hard, and when it was finished, Jeff hoped he'd never have to do it again.

All the time the vegetable cleanup was in process, Jeff worried about Rinda's illness and Pera's lack of response to Norby's attempts to reach her telepathically.

When Norby came down from lifting the last load to the airtruck, he announced, "Job complete, Officer Luka." He also touched Jeff's hand and spoke telepathically.

—I've been trying to reach Pera and I can't. It's as if she's vanished from the whole planet!

—There must be some explanation, Norby. We'll find out.

"Now," said Luka, "I will take you to the queen for sentencing. I must warn you that she is not in a good mood."

Yobo mumbled, "Is she ever?" but Luka paid no attention.

"Leave your ship where it is. There is very little traffic near the palace this week. Everyone is at the fair."

10

"To see me," said a different voice.

A fantastic figure was leaning nonchalantly against the outer rim of the police car's airlock. The traditional baggy pants and upper tunic worn by Izzians were modified into a one-piece garment made of diamond shapes, black interspersed with motley color sections sewn with spangles. The man wore a sleek silver helmet surmounted by an elongated gold diamond with a sharp upper point, and his long pigtail was tied with spangled red ribbon. Even his black boots were festooned with gold bands.

"Hello, Ing, you ingrate," Yobo said.

"What is an 'ingrate'?" asked Luka.

"A term of affection, my dear," said Ing, shifting position so his body seemed to iridesce. Jeff reflected that harlequins might have worn the colors, the diamond shapes, and the spangles, but not the baggy pants. Then he saw that the black diamonds were actually holes cut in the garment, showing a skintight black body suit Ing wore underneath.

"I'll bet you egged Luka on to arrest us," Yobo said in Terran Basic. "We'll see about that." He shifted to Izzian. "Officer, I demand that audience with the queen. It offends my Martian dignity to talk to the court fool."

"His what dignity?" asked Luka, clearly bewildered.

"Never mind, love. I'll go on to the fair, you take the intruders to the queen, see if you can have them put in jail, and I'll meet you later after my performance."

"Yes, Ing. I hate to miss any of your shows. Take my ship over to the fair. I'll go by subcar."

"Ta-ta, Terrans. It is too bad you'll be incarcerated. My act is the best thing at the fair. But you'll be able to catch my regular show on holov at the prison."

At this moment a passing Izzian family spied Ing waving at Admiral Yobo and rushed over, demanding autographs. Ing gave them, looking up to leer at Yobo and Jeff from time to time. At last the family was satisfied and, with a kiss blown to Luka, Ing went back in the ship and took off.

11

As the police aircar flew over the *Pride*, the airlock opened and a small round object fell out. It looked like a red balloon, only balloons aren't supposed to fall. It landed on Yobo's ship, broke, and splattered paint on the top.

With Yobo grinding his teeth behind him, Jeff watched the police ship fly on, over the city square and its spectacular gardens, over the low office buildings on the other side, and toward a huge gleaming dome beyond. He could just make out a door opening in the dome and Ing's vehicle entering.

"That's a beautiful dome," Jeff said.

"Izzhall is our most impressive building, after the palace," said Luka, raising her gun again. "In the daytime the auditorium is used by the elected Izzian Council members, who obey the queen's orders and give advice, when ordered."

"Not exactly a democracy around here," said Yobo.

"No, Admiral," said Norby, nudging Jeff. "Much more like Space Command."

"That will do, Cadet Robot."

"Yes, sir."

"Why is Ing going to the Izzian Council?" asked Jeff.

"The council does not meet in Fair Week," Luka said. "During the year, Izzhall is used at night for special spectacles too big to fit in the usual theaters and concert halls. But when Fair Week arrives, the entire structure of Izzhall is filled with booths for the toy and game manufacturers to display their products, and an open auditorium for performances. Ing, our marvelous court jester, is the most popular performer."

"I'll bet," said Yobo. "Once that villain decided to be a clown, he turned on charm that no doubt gets him just what he wants—like the use of a police car."

"I don't know what you mean," Luka said stiffly. "Ing is a revered citizen of Izz, a celebrity everyone wants to know. It is only natural that the chief of police make every effort to protect and—and to serve him. March on, to the queen."

Yobo, Jeff, and Norby trudged up the steps in front of

Luka's gun. On either side of the massive, gold-paneled front door stood a robot twice as tall as Yobo. Each robot was only vaguely humanoid, with stumpy legs holding up a huge cylinder of a body from which emerged jointed arms and a small, sensor-rimmed head devoid of personality.

"They look like walking garbage cans," said Norby, who was proud of his own small barrel shape.

"Be careful, little robot," said Luka, "or I will instruct a guard to put you inside its holding cell."

"Its *body*? That's indecent."

"Not at all. These guard robots protect the royal family, keep order at the fair, and are under my command to keep the peace of Izz. March on!"

Far away from the Terran Federation and home, Jeff and his two friends marched into the palace.

—Jeff, I have the distinct impression that Luka's in love with the court jester.

—I'm afraid so, Norby. And look at the admiral—he's so mad he's coming to the boil. I'm worried . . .

—So am I. If we can't find Pera, and can't see Rinda, who on Izz will stand up for us?

3.

Queen Tizzle of Izz

"Straight ahead to the throne room," Luka said. "And don't dillydally. I want to get this over with quickly so I can see Ing's performance at the fair."

"Ing! A court jester! Bah!" The hardening of Yobo's jaw made it look like black steel.

"Ing is an important personage." Luka fell back to be in line with Yobo. She smiled radiantly. "Such a marvelous court jester, and naturally he's also master of ceremonies at the fair. And he's so modest."

"Modest? That megalomaniac scoundrel?"

"Why, yes. He didn't even tell you that in addition to being court jester and master of ceremonies, he invented a popular game called Teenytrip and another called Ballsaway. He is so talented that now he's been made court scientist."

"I thought Izz had a court scientist."

"The previous one married and retired to a farm at the other end of Izzcontinent. The queen asked Ing to be court scientist because he seems to know more about technology than Izzian scientists, who confine themselves to theoretical study, not practical applications."

"That, my dear Luka, is because the Others wanted Izz to be peaceful and prosperous. They filled the cities with ultramodern technology that repairs itself. You Izzians didn't have to invent your way out of primitive life, the way we humans did who were left on Earth."

"We Izzians don't invent anything but toys and games, and a few external improvements in our vehicles and homes. The Others taught our ancestors how to keep the population

14

stable, so we live comfortably in complete peace and prosperity."

Jeff noticed the frown on Luka's attractive forehead. "Officer Luka, is there something wrong here in Izz?"

"Prosperity has declined somewhat lately. Nobody knows why. Presumably the queen is attending to the matter."

"If Ing's involved in your Izzian problems, you can say goodbye to peace and prosperity," Yobo said.

They had reached a set of double doors guarded by two purple-draped robots of conventional size. Luka saluted them and paused. "Now don't upset the queen. She's having enough problems without three non-Izzians giving her trouble. And don't say nasty things about Ing. He's a favorite of the royal family and does his best to cheer them up."

Yobo's eyebrows raised. "I'd bet that Ing's trying to take over the country. Up to his old tricks."

Luka laughed. "You forget—Izz is a matriarchy. Only females can run the country. Males occasionally complain about it, but they never get anywhere."

The double doors swung inward and the robots shouted: "Hail to the queen." Luka shoved Jeff and Yobo into the throne room. Norby held Jeff's hand as they approached the massive gold throne occupied by a tall woman wearing a gold crown on her unbraided brown hair.

—I remember the queen's face as fierce, Jeff, but now she just looks anxious. I wonder why? And where's the king? His throne is empty.

—Norby, try tilting a little forward on your feet, so it will seem as if you're bowing. Even the admiral is bowing. Remember that we're in trouble.

—I'll take the blame. It wasn't your or the admiral's fault that we hit the truck.

—I'll take the blame. I'll say I was driving. We can't take the risk of having the Pool of Plurf deactivate you.

—We have only a week's vacation and it will take longer for plurf to wear off you, Jeff. And what if she decides that the admiral, being the oldest, is in charge and has to be dunked too? I can just see the two of you spending weeks in the ship because you can't go back to Space Command . . .

Jeff was suddenly conscious that Yobo's hand was on his shoulder and that he'd therefore been able to tune into the telepathic conversation.

—Norby, Jeff—let me handle this and we won't have to worry about plurf.

Yobo strode past Luka and bowed magnificently, every inch the descendant of African kings. This effect was rather spoiled by the fact that when his head lifted his face registered the kind of biological shock likely to occur when a man is surprised by the sight of extraordinary female beauty.

It was not the queen who had caused Yobo's previously tight jaw to drop, his eyes to open wider, and his nostrils to flare.

While Luka had been herding her charges toward the queen, a girl had entered the throne room from a back door. She now stood near the throne, her hands clasped in front of her simple white tunic, her large dark eyes placidly clear, her red lips smooth and soft in her perfectly shaped, creamy-brown face. She was small and slim, wearing her brown braid pinned in a coil by a gold clasp set with a green stone. She was lovely.

" 'Was this the face that launch'd a thousand ships and burnt the topless towers of Ilium?' " Yobo said in English.

Jeff agreed wholeheartedly with Marlowe's ancient question, but since the queen was staring at Yobo's sudden fixation on the newcomer, the situation was getting out of control.

The girl's face was so riveting that they hadn't noticed she'd come in with a companion, a tall, gloweringly handsome young man. He stood nearby, spots of red on each pale cheekbone, his two black braids disheveled and the sleeves of his green tunic pushed up as if he were getting ready for a fight. Or had already been in one.

16

The queen of Izz sighed, rose to her feet, and said, "Well, Luka, can't you see I'm busy?"

Stammering a little, Luka explained about the airtruck.

"My daughter has informed me that she witnessed the accident from her tower, and that you arrested her friends, after they kindly picked up the vegetables." The queen managed a wan smile at Yobo, Jeff, and Norby. "Welcome to Izz, again. I hope all is well with your Terran Federation."

"No more trouble than usual, Your Queenness," Yobo said smoothly, having recovered from seeing the girl, perhaps easier for a man rather more than a little involved with the Federation's prime minister, a beauty in her own right.

The queen bent forward to stare at Yobo. "Your regrettable lack of head hair . . ."

Jeff held his breath.

"Is made up for by the perfection of your moustache."

"Thank you, ma'am," Yobo said. "We have come to Izz to attend your famous toy and game fair, but since we in the Federation are used to coping with troubles and solving problems, we offer our services. We are yours to command."

"Indeed," said the queen, tapping her chin meditatively. "You are most kind."

"Your Queenness, about these prisoners . . ."

"You have done your duty, Luka," said the queen with a gesture of dismissal. "Return to the fair to keep order there, and I will attend to my *guests*."

Luka winced. "Yes, Your Queenness."

"And Luka, watch out for the Jylot delegation."

Luka was obviously astonished. "Jylot? But they never come to Izzcontinent. They stay on their islands."

"Until now. I have received word that a delegation of them is going to the fair this afternoon. As the only native life-form left on Izz, they are unpredictably primitive."

"But they've always traded their sea-harvest for our goods in the most peaceful way," Luka said. "What has happened?"

"I have heard that they are angry about certain toys."

"But the Jylot don't use toys."

The handsome young man stepped forward. "Your majesty, one of the new soft toys is shaped like a Jylot. I demonstrate this toy at the fair and it is extremely popular."

The queen said, "Please cease the demonstrations, Garus. The first visit of the Jylot must be pleasant and peaceful."

"The trouble is that already many people have bought the toy and will be carrying them at the fair. The Jylot delegation will undoubtedly notice . . ."

"I understand," the queen said tiredly. "You might as well go ahead with the demonstration, but try to be dignified and for Izz's sake don't do anything with the toy Jylot that could possibly offend the originals. Luka, go with Garus and make sure there isn't a riot. I don't want anyone hurt."

"We will go to the fair at once, Your Queenness. Come with me, Garus."

"Sure thing, Luka," said the young man named Garus, who then turned to the beautiful young woman. "Xeena, will you please not forget that we're singing at the fair this afternoon? That is, if I can stop Ing from hogging the limelight and making passes at you."

Luka's mouth tightened at this, and she said, apparently through clenched teeth, "Ing is interested in you, Xeena?"

The girl named Xeena had long eyelashes that seemed to droop over her eyes when she looked sad. "I'm sure he only wants me in his toy fair act, but I already have so much to do—singing in our holov show, and trying to learn how to be assistant court scientist."

The queen frowned. "Xeena, you achieved the highest science grades in school, which is why I selected you to learn practical science from Ing. Your singing talents are good, but perhaps you are trying to do too much."

"It's Ing who's doing too much," Garus said belligerently. "He's not only court scientist, court jester, and the fair's master of ceremonies, but he also runs the holov station and won't let me have my own show, with Xeena."

For an instant the queen's eyes twinkled. "I suppose you think you'd be a better court jester, too?"

Garus's elegant nose went into the air. "Certainly not. I have no desire to give up serious drama to be stuck in a stuffy palace."

Luka drew her breath in sharply, and even Yobo looked alarmed, for the queen of Izz was not given to accepting insults with equanimity. Yet when the queen spoke, it was with sardonic amusement rather than anger.

"Garus, if you could make a living at serious drama, you wouldn't have taken a job demonstrating products at a toy fair. Take him back to the fair, Luka. I have matters to discuss with Xeena and with my guests."

When Luka and Garus had left, the queen turned to Xeena. "So Ing's falling in love with you, is he?"

"I don't—I mean—I haven't—"

"Don't hang your head, girl. With a face like yours it's not your fault. How quickly can you learn practical science from Ing, Xeena?"

"Well, it's true that Ing seems to know a great deal, but he's not very good at teaching it, and then Garus resents the time I'm with anyone else . . ."

"I should think so."

". . . but I'm not officially engaged to Garus, and I do like my singing and acting career, too. Perhaps we Izzians have no talent for technology, Your Queenness."

"Nonsense," Yobo said. "Anybody with brains can learn anything, and you clearly have brains, Xeena. Much more than Earth's Helen of Troy, who also captured men's hearts."

Xeena blinked. "On his holov show, Ing has told many legends of ancient Earth, including those of the Trojan war. I think Helen was wicked to leave her husband in Sparta to go with the Trojan Paris. Then she just sat there in Troy

19

while the Greeks and Trojans fought a war over her for ten years."

"Jeff and I like best the part where Ulysses sneaks the Greek soldiers into Troy inside a wooden horse," Norby piped up. "That's more exciting than the fuss over Helen."

"I don't think Ing has told that story," said Xeena.

"None of the soldiers were female," said Norby. "In those days females didn't have much spunk."

Xeena hung her head again, as if embarrassed about the fact that she was not a typical Izzian female, the dominant sex. Jeff thought she seemed more like Helen of Troy than she knew.

The queen said, "On Izz females are raised to have strength, determination, and power. It is part of our tradition. The rulers of Izz are always from a line of royal female descendants. The males of the royal line are fortunate, because they are free to pursue their own interests . . ."

A disembodied voice interrupted the queen. "Well, just because Garus is pursuing Xeena is no reason for my friends Jeff and Admiral Yobo to do the same!"

4.

Royal Troubles

The queen's holov screen shimmered, shook, and resolved to a view of a bed, upon which sat a green-clad figure with red hair and a veil over her face. Jeff smiled, for unlike Xeena, the eleven-year-old crown princess of Izz was not only spunky but positively feisty.

"Furthermore," Rinda continued from beneath the veil, "I am annoyed that Jeff and the admiral did not bother to call me the instant they arrived in Izz."

"As you saw, we had a slight, ah, traffic problem arriving at your lovely planet, Princess," said Yobo, with a slight bow to the holov screen. "It has only now been resolved."

"My husband and daughter are in quarantine for ickyspot," said the queen. "Fortunately, I've had it. Poor Fizzy, being an adult, has a bad case, but you are almost well, Rinda. Take off that silly veil or I'll think the doctors are wrong about your being able to join your friends tomorrow."

"But I'm still spotty! I don't want Jeff to see me!"

"I don't mind. You'll always look good to me, Rinda." Saying that in the same room with a veritable Helen of Troy, Jeff knew it was true.

The face veil came off. To Jeff, Rinda's face seemed thinner and more sophisticated, in spite of the spattering of spots. She was growing up.

"It's a light case of ickyspot, Jeff," Rinda said. "If you've had it you could visit me now."

"Jeff is my responsibility," said Yobo. "I can't permit him to visit you in person, Princess. Neither he nor I have had ickyspot. We in the Federation are immunized in childhood

21

against all of our contagious diseases, but ickyspot may be unique to Izzians. Jeff and I have to be careful because we must return to our duties."

"Oh, I guess I can wait until tomorrow," Rinda said, "but I hate missing the fair. I wanted to see Xeena and cousin Garus perform."

"Cousin?" asked Norby.

"A very distant relative," said the queen. "Garus is descended through royal males from my great-great-uncle Orz."

"Who was the rightful heir," said Rinda. "He didn't want to be king—there was no one to be queen—so he abdicated and was succeeded by his younger brother Narrin, Mother's great-great-grandfather, who produced a daughter Narra, who produced Narriza, my grandmother."

"Garus has no claim to the throne," said the queen. "Orz's first wife divorced him, and his second had only a son, who had a son named Orran, Garus's father—the ranger for our nature sanctuary, Wildpark."

"I wish I could take you to Wildpark, Jeff," said Rinda. "You'd like it."

"Maybe we'll have time to go there after you're well."

—Now we know [Norby said telepathically to Jeff] why Garus can say pretty much what he wants around the queen. But Jeff, why hasn't anyone noticed that Pera is missing?

As if in answer to Norby's silent question, Rinda said, "Has anyone seen Pera? She went on an errand a couple of hours ago and hasn't come back."

The queen bent forward to stare at the holov screen. "My dear, I'm sure Pera will return. There's no need to get so agitated about it."

Indeed, Rinda's hands seemed to be twitching slightly.

"I'm not agitated, I'm just asking . . . Why are all of you staring at me as if I'm crazy?"

Rinda's left shoulder had begun to twitch violently. The

22

queen gasped and said, "My daughter! Send the physicians . . ."

"What's the matter?" asked Rinda. "I feel fine."

"You're twitching," said Jeff. "Is that one of the symptoms of ickyspot?"

"No," said the queen. "Rinda, you're having spasms . . ."

"I'm *not*, but *your* holov image is, Mother! Your mouth quirks up in a horrible sneer, the way it did when you spoke on holov this morning. That's what I sent Pera to investigate at the holov station."

Jeff touched Norby. —Rinda's sick. Don't tell her Pera asked for help and is now out of contact.

Norby said, "Princess, Pera must have noticed what no human could perceive—that when your royal images twitch, there's a faint glitch in the entire holov screen. Since your bodies are not actually twitching, the fault must be in the holov transmission."

The queen nodded. "Pera is a good little robot. I'm sorry to admit it, but I need help. Izz needs help. Our businesses have recently been so plagued by mysterious malfunctions and failures that our economy is on the verge of disaster. The people are distressed and tend to blame me."

Xeena stepped forward. "I will do what I can to help, Your Queenness. I will go to the holov station and confer with the robot Pera and, of course, with Court Scientist Ing."

"Do so," said the queen. "The holov transmission must be repaired before tomorrow. It is Affirmation Day, when the elected Izzcouncil asks the Mainbrain who is the rightful ruler of Izz. My name is always given, and if my image is made to sneer, the people may decide to reject me."

"What is the Mainbrain?" asked Yobo.

"The main computer that correlates the entire Izzian computer system."

Yobo frowned. "In the Federation, we have many computer systems, integrated now but with fail-safe design. Do

23

you have only one system, and only one controlling computer?"

"That is correct. The Others installed it, millennia ago, and put the Mainbrain in a sealed vault because it does not need repair or major program changes. Minor alterations in programming are performed through individual terminals, but the holov station is almost entirely separate. Problems in holov transmission must come from the station."

"Your majesty," said Yobo, "I would like permission to accompany Xeena. I know that the royal family approves of Ing, but I don't trust him. I'd like to see what he does at the holov station."

"And I can work with Pera," said Norby. "I'll go, too. But first, may I plug myself into your computer terminal, Queen Tizzle? I would like to scan the Mainbrain. Perhaps it has a record of malfunctions."

"Go ahead," said the queen.

"What an amazing robot," said Xeena. "We have nothing like him on Izz."

"Except Pera," said Norby, plugging himself in. "But I'm better at computer scanning than she is . . ."

"What's the matter, Norby?" asked Jeff.

"Odd. I can't scan the Mainbrain at all."

The queen shrugged. "I told you the Mainbrain was totally sealed. Remember that the first humans brought to Izz were completely primitive. The advanced technological civilization they were given had to be protected from them."

"But you've never learned enough about your computer system to help it control the technology you've developed over the years—like the holov station," said Norby.

"That is true," the queen said sadly. "Perhaps that is because the rulers have always been female. Some of the discontented male citizens say that kings would have done more with our technology."

"Nonsense, Mother," said Rinda. "I'm a girl and I'm much

24

more interested in computer science than cousin Garus, who's set on being a great actor."

"Ing is an actor," Yobo said slowly. "As well as being proficient with computers, and with putting holov to his own nefarious uses."

5.

Izzbroadcasting

On orders from the queen, Xeena led the Federation visitors out of the throne room to the nearest antigrav lift. They descended to the palace sub-basement where they entered a gleaming subcar that shot through underground tunnels toward the holov station beneath Izzhall.

The admiral was still brooding about Ing. "As court scientist, court jester, holov station manager, and toy fair master of ceremonies, Ing is in charge of a great deal of important work, which is all located in the same place. Doesn't this bother anybody, Xeena?"

"To most Izzians, work is trivial, for hard work is done mainly by robots, computers, and of course the queen. Izzians are preoccupied with play. Ing is admired for his cleverness in providing year-round holov entertainment and for making this year's toy and game fair the most successful in history. In your Federation, do you not believe in play?"

"We believe in *work*."

Norby chortled with tinny sarcasm, for the admiral was known for his succession of hobbies and assorted extracurricular interests. But, thought Jeff, it was true that when Yobo worked, he drove himself just as hard as he drove others.

Yobo said, "Work seems like play if you like it."

Xeena nodded. "Ing also says one can be creatively playful in any kind of work. He certainly enjoys his jobs as court jester and holov station manager. I'm not sure about his job as court scientist. That seems to bore him."

"Perhaps because however much he knows about science

and technology, Ing doesn't enjoy that work as much as he likes being the center of attention. A court scientist should work hard at it."

"Oh, dear," Xeena said. "I couldn't do that."

"Never you mind, Helen of Troy. With a smile like yours, no reason you should have to work at anything."

—Jeff, Yobo's male chauvinism is rising high.

—She's very beautiful.

—That last smile of hers was aimed at you, Jeff. Perhaps you can win out over the admiral, Garus, and Ing.

—I don't want to. I like Rinda.

Aloud, Jeff said, "Xeena, Ing must have done some scientific work, because Officer Luka said he's invented two popular games. Are they displayed at the fair?"

"Yes. Few items are actually for sale, but one can buy Ing's popular Teenytrip and Ballsaway. But be sure to see Garus display the Jylot dolls. Garus"—Xeena's satin cheeks deepened in color—"is much nicer than he seems."

"How did you meet him?" asked Jeff.

"A year ago we were both performing in a musical play. After we became friends, Garus occasionally took me to visit his parents on the island of Wildpark. It is accessible by aircar, but one must park only in designated places, for beyond the recreation area and the ranger's house, there is only wilderness. Neither Wildpark nor the Jylot-inhabited islands have any electrical connection to the mainland. The ranger's electricity is beamed from the solar satellites."

"Wildpark sounds great. It must get very crowded," said Jeff, remembering some of the parks on Earth.

"Oh, no. Izzians prefer civilization, and there are other, more luxurious park areas right on the continent. It was highly unusual for Garus's great-grandfather Orz to abdicate the throne in order to become a Wildpark ranger."

"Since Izzians don't like hard work," Yobo said with disapproval, "it's no wonder he didn't want to rule Izz, which seems to be a tough job."

"The queen does indeed have to work very hard," said Xeena, "but perhaps she likes the power."

The subcar came to a halt at an immense gold-plated station labeled "Izzhall," where tunnels converged from many sectors. It was crowded with people using escalators to get up to the fair. Xeena headed for an underground corridor that ended at double doors labeled "Izzbroadcasting."

Norby rose on antigrav to Jeff's chest. "Hold me, Jeff. I'm going to concentrate on locating Pera." When Jeff's arms went around Norby, the little robot shut both pairs of eyes and extended his sensor wire from his hat.

Inside the station, kinetic activity centered around Ing, busy rehearsing and telling everyone everywhere what to do. He did not notice when Norby sailed out of Jeff's arms to explore the entire station on his own.

Garus ran over to Xeena, but Ing instantly joined the group and started to yell at him.

"When you hold the Jylot doll, you idiot, act as if it's a cute baby animal everyone will want to buy. Remember that you're not emoting in drama, you're trying to persuade customers and please manufacturers. Ah—Xeena, my love, my little nightingale. Show our visitors how well we sing together."

"I'm supposed to sing with Xeena!" Garus shouted. "We've always sung the love duets. You've hogged the funny commercials on Teenytrip and Ballsaway, but remember you're only a jester. Don't get too uppity with a real actor-singer like me, because I have more clout with the royal family."

Ing clenched his fists and muttered something insulting about inadequate actors and arrogant royal relatives.

Yobo chuckled and quoted: " 'There are one or two rules, half a dozen maybe, that all family fools, of whatever degree, must observe, *must* observe if they love their profession.' "

Ing's fists clenched. "Boris, my old nemesis, little do you

realize what you did in exiling me to this Gilbert-and-Sullivan planet of Izz, where nobody minds how I suffer, just as long as I'm funny."

"Speaking of being funny, Ing," said Yobo, "just how far have you gone in 'plying your craft, aiming your shaft at prince and peer'? There've been some not-so-funny things going on around here . . ."

" 'I aim my shaft and know no fear!' " sang Ing. "There are indeed compensations to being a court jester. Royal families, including the various withered branches thereof, are good targets when you're paid to be funny." He leered at Xeena. "Go ahead and sing with the young royal lout, but don't get too mushy about it."

Garus picked up a stringed instrument, strummed, and sang:

"Buy a Jylot, pretty lady, buy a Jylot so sweet,
I assure you, pretty lady, that it makes life complete."

After a preliminary giggle, Xeena's answered in her soft soprano:

"Good sir, I will try one, if you show me how,
Does its softness take the tension away from my
brow?"

Admiral Yobo moaned slightly. "I've always loathed singing commercials, Ing. Can't you do better than that?"

"Anything—almost anything the traffic will allow, chum." Ing showed his teeth again at Xeena and Garus. "You'll do, I suppose. Now we must get to the fair. Hurry, minions. Our stage awaits."

Garus turned to go, but Xeena stepped up to Yobo with an enchanting smile that caused her two suitors to frown. "First I must beg a favor from you, Admiral."

29

"I hope that you want me to instruct you in science, Xeena. It doesn't look as if you'll be learning much of that from a court jester."

"Ah, Xeena," Ing said, blowing her a kiss. "Would you rather study instead of reveling in a well-turned phrase, capturing love in a melody, and conjuring up the best of creations—wild applause?"

"At the moment I don't want to study. I just want to touch the admiral's amazing head."

"What's amazing about that head?" Ing snapped.

"It is so smooth. I have never seen a head like it."

"It's *bald!*" Ing yelled. "A deficiency . . ."

Yobo expanded his chest and smiled at Xeena, ignoring the glares from both Ing and Garus. "I am honored by your request, dear Xeena. In my solar system, bald heads are revered." Yobo glanced sideways at Jeff as if daring him to disagree, and then he bent low so that Xeena could touch the top of his head.

"So interesting." Xeena caressed Yobo's head rather tentatively, as if a bald head were almost frightening.

"Watch it, Yobo," Ing said in Terran Basic. "Leave that female alone. We Izzians claim first dibs on her beauty."

"We Izzians?" Yobo said in Terran Basic as he straightened up. "You watch it, too, Ing. You've got your fingers in too many Izzian pies. Stick to jestering, but you'd better stop making too much fun of the royal family or I may bake you in one of your pies."

"I have no idea what you're talking about," said Ing, taking Xeena's shapely arm. Garus instantly took the other just as Norby floated back into the main control room.

"Jealous males around Helen of Troy," Norby commented. "Ing, that's a hackneyed plot."

"Did you find any trace of Pera?" asked Jeff.

"She's not in the station. I'll plug into the computer system here . . ."

"What is that robot doing?!" Ing cried, pointing at Norby.

"Queen's orders," said Yobo. "We're trying to find what's wrong here at the station."

"Nothing's wrong," said Ing. "How could there be when I'm in charge?"

"Hah!" said Yobo. "Do you deny you're responsible for the unpleasant twitches in the images of the royal family?"

Ing shrugged. "Now that you mention it, I have noticed an amusing phenomenon that appears now and then when the queen's on-screen. But I assure you the fault must be in the palace, not here."

"Neither," Norby said, disconnecting. "The computers at the palace and here in the holov station are not at fault. They are merely passing along errors that start someplace else, I'm not sure where, since I can't explore the Mainbrain to track down the source."

"Suppose the Mainbrain itself is going bad?" asked Jeff. "After all, it's been working without repairs for millennia."

Ing laughed. "All Izzian civilization depends on the Mainbrain's integrity. I know plenty about computers, and I'm sure everything's hunky-dory. The glitch isn't from here."

"Did you see the glitch that just happened?" asked Norby.

"What glitch?" said Ing. "I was speaking metaphorically."

"In that monitor over there. Not a distortion of the queen's face, but during a newsbreak when stockmarket prices were being quoted."

"That couldn't be a glitch. Prices change," said Ing.

"This number was in a column, and the sum did not change, it merely became incorrect. As far as I've been able to find out so far, there are occasional random errors appearing in the computer system. This is more than just a holov problem affecting the queen's broadcasts. Even a small random numerical error could play havoc with the Izzian economy, since it's so tightly interwoven."

"I don't understand," said Xeena, looking bewildered.

"Come on," Garus said, pulling her, "this isn't important. We don't want to be late at the fair."

"You understand these mysterious errors, don't you, Ing?" asked Yobo.

"Not at all. It has nothing to do with me. I'm going to the fair with Xeena and Garus. Just don't demolish the holov station while I'm gone."

"Ing!" shouted Yobo. "You're a scientist and a schemer as well as a jester. You'd better stay here and undo the damage you've already done to Izz."

"Damage? All I've done is get rich on my incredible theatrical talent, and my games—come to the fair and buy 'em. You'll like 'em. I agree with the Izzian philosophy—play games and ignore the glitches."

"Izz has been going downhill since you arrived on the planet," Yobo said. "Pretending you're just a jester . . ."

Shooing Garus and Xeena ahead of him, Ing pranced to the door singing, " 'A jester fair to see, a pearl of ribaldry . . .' "

"Ing!"

The court jester paused in the doorway. "Oh, by the way, old baldy, I don't intend to trouble myself over the troubles of Izz. I wouldn't mind being an Einstein, and I'd have loved being Genghis Khan—and almost was, in one of my former roles—but believe me, Boris, there's no perfect business except show business, to coin a phrase. Ta-ta."

Ing had vanished, leaving the holov station curiously quiet. An underling came up to the three Federation visitors and asked if there was anything they wanted.

"Yes," said Norby. "The robot Pera, who belongs to the crown princess, came here this morning. What happened to her?"

"To Ing's annoyance, she pried into our computers. Then she said the trouble was elsewhere, and before we could find out what she was talking about, she left. Somebody said they saw her at the fair."

"Are there computers at the fair?" asked Jeff.

The underling's eyebrows shot up. "Three-fourths of the

toys displayed at the fair are computerized, and almost all of the games. Everything on Izz is run by computer, especially the fair itself, so naturally there are big terminals there."

"And ways of programming the computer system?" asked Jeff.

"The main computer system's hardware and much of the software are permanent, and no major programming alterations can be made, only superficial changes like those necessary to create new games, update consumer goods, and alter holov entertainment."

"Your holov transmission was altered, humiliating the queen," Yobo said angrily. "Or are you in on this with Ing?"

The underling, a small, wispy man, backed away from Yobo. "Ing told us to search for faulty transmission, but we've found nothing. There's no malfunction here."

"No," said Norby. "If there's a malfunction, it has to be in the Mainbrain itself."

"If, Norby?" asked Jeff. "As opposed to . . ."

"To deliberate sabotage."

"That's what I've been saying all along," said Yobo. "Ing is trying to destroy Izz so he can take over."

"But even I can't get into the Mainbrain," said Norby. "So how is Ing doing all that he's doing?"

"We'll go to that blasted fair to see him in action," said Yobo. "Ing and his games, forsooth!

"Norby," Yobo went on slowly, "Pera called you for help. Could she have called while she was here in the station or after she went to the fair to see Ing?"

Norby closed his eyes for a second. When they opened he said, "I don't know, but we came to Izz immediately, so it's possible that she called from the fair."

The wispy underling sidled nearer to Jeff. "Going to the fair, are you? Supposed to be change."

"What do you mean, change?"

"We'll know tomorrow, won't we? You have tried the game, haven't you?" He picked up a small, bright red box labeled "Teenytrip" and trotted from the room.

6.

The Toy and Game Fair

The walls beside the escalators were covered by holoscenes advertising food (from iced Izzade to fried figgis); fashion (how to have the baggiest pants in town); and recreation (mainly ocean cruises or trips to Wildpark).

"Lucky Garus, growing up in Wildpark," Jeff said. In the holoscene, tall trees let through a leaf-filtered light that played on giant ferns dotting the forest floor.

"I prefer cities," said Norby, "with lots of electricity so I can recharge without going into hyperspace. The holov station's juice was as tasty as any I've found."

The escalator disgorged them into a huge lobby. Doors to the outside were at their right, and to the left was a series of golden archways. Over the arches were Izzian letters saying "Each Part of the All," the slogan of the Izzian government.

"Not true," muttered Yobo. "Izzian citizens are not at all part of their own government. The queen does everything."

"The queen and the robots. Look at them," said Norby.

Huge robots like those at the palace guarded each archway. They were so intimidating that Jeff took Norby's hand as they walked under an arch into the main floor of Izzhall. The danger, however, was from something much smaller.

"Hey, Mom! Look at the cute robot—I want one!"

Norby drew his other arm into his body before the little boy grabbed it. "You can't buy me!"

"Nonsense—you're just a toy," said the mother, an Izzian lady of dimensions and vocal powers to rival those of the queen. "How much?" she asked Jeff.

"This robot belongs to me and is not for sale." Fending off

two aggressive little girls, Jeff and Norby retreated behind Yobo's bulk as the woman marched determinedly toward him and a crowd collected around the group.

The admiral's bass roared out. "Madam, cease and desist!"

"Get out of my way! I'll have the authorities on you for being carelessly and hairlessly unbraided!"

"Madam, notice the meticulous braiding of my moustache, done in honor of our fair queen, by whose special consent I am allowed to be hairless above."

The crowd gave a collective gasp of astonishment.

"Furthermore," Yobo continued, "please remove your child from the vicinity of our experimental robot, which if touched the wrong way may explode."

"In anger," Norby said softly to Jeff.

As the crowd melted back to create a small space around Norby, the mother sniffed and pulled her offspring away from his attempts to secure a handhold on Norby. "Not now, dear. After things change, perhaps I'll buy you a safe version of that robot." Mother and child left.

"Yeah," said an older boy, who had been gazing covetously at Norby. "After the change."

"What change?" asked Jeff.

"Tomorrow. Everybody's expecting it. Don't you know about it? Haven't you played the game?"

"I don't know what you're talking about."

"We'll all find out tomorrow. Just wait. With change, we'll all get what we want." The boy drifted away.

"Something funny's going on," Yobo said. "Norby, you walk between Jeff and me. There are hordes of children here."

"I can always escape by going up in the air . . ."

"You'll get in trouble, Norby," said Jeff. "Look at the sign over there—no miniantigrav units to be operated in Izzhall."

"I'll escape into hyperspace."

Yobo shook his head. "Better not, if you can help it. We don't want the Izzians to know how many talents you have.

35

At least at the moment people aren't crowding us. We have a chance to look for Pera."

"I can't detect her presence. I don't think she's here," Norby said in his tinniest, most discouraged voice. "She can't escape into hyperspace, so maybe some horrible child grabbed her and she's trapped at someone's home right now."

"But if that were the case," Jeff said, "she'd be able to call you telepathically, and since you're now on Izz you'd hear, wouldn't you?"

"That's right. Where can she be? Has some even more horrible adolescent deactivated her?"

"Now, boys," said Yobo, "let's reconnoiter Izzhall and make certain she's not here. And at the same time try to find out what the people mean when they talk about change."

"Did you notice their eyes, Admiral?" Jeff said. "Most of them had an odd look, as if they're drugged but quite awake."

"We ought to tell the queen about this. There's Officer Luka." Yobo strode over to Luka, who was standing by a large platform erected at one side of the hall. The other sides were plastered with booths selling food and souvenirs, while the central section of the hall was divided by sound-absorbing partitions into a maze of different displays of toys and games, each presided over by a human actor who demonstrated his or her wares to whatever audience had entered that partitioned space.

"Officer Luka, we're concerned about the people here in Izzhall," Yobo said in his most official manner. "They look as if what they've been eating or drinking here has been drugged, and they keep talking about change."

"Well, of course there's going to be change," said Luka impatiently. "This is the last day of the fair. Tomorrow is Affirmation Day. Izzhall will be very different then."

"Someone mentioned playing a game in connection with the change," Jeff said. "What game is that?"

"I don't know," said Luka. "I don't have time to play games. I'm too busy protecting the master of ceremonies."

"From what?" asked Yobo.

"His many fans." Luka's disapproval was obvious. "They pull off his spangles as souvenirs and beg him to write limericks for them. I have to make sure he's able to give his performance unmolested. Fame is so exhausting for poor Ing."

"I'll bet," Yobo said. "When's his next act?"

"Soon. If you walk along that aisle over there, you'll find Garus at his exhibit, demonstrating Jylot dolls."

Yobo, Jeff, and Norby wound through the aisles until they came to the Jylot dolls. Garus was holding one for display.

"Gentlefolk," Garus said, "you have never seen or felt any toy so guaranteed to give soothing comfort and silent companionship as this Jylot doll. It is an exact replica of an actual Jylot, but softer, more cuddly. Enjoy it, folks!"

As the spiel went on, Jeff found himself almost wanting to buy a Jylot, although he felt that fifteen-year-olds were beyond needing a stuffed animal toy. Slightly bigger than housecats, the Jylot dolls were shaped like lumpy eggs whose thicker end balanced on two stubby webbed feet. Around what was presumably the waist grew a circlet of six ropy tentacles. At what might be called the neck area was a fringe of gill-like slits on either side of an ovoid mouth. Above this was another circlet of six tiny, fringed blue eyes. The Jylot's pelt was blue hair, as short as velvet.

So persuasive were Garus and the doll's appearance that almost every child brought into the demonstration area went out with an imitation Jylot.

"Where's Xeena?" Yobo asked Garus.

"Six booths on, demonstrating Teenytrips," said Garus. "Go see her and then come to hear us sing."

They walked past assorted games and toys, many of them

much like those for sale in the Federation. They laughed at the "Monster" game, complete with costumes for participants, because the Izzian idea of alien monsters could not compare with those dreamed up on Earth. Roboticized human baby dolls were boring, since they'd been around Earth for centuries, but Jeff liked the Freezem Gun, which made tiny holoimages of whatever you shot at and imbedded them in plastic balls.

The display called "Ballsaway, a hand-held game of skill invented by Ing" brought a guffaw from Yobo. "Look at that, will you! It's nothing but a crude version of one of those ancient Terran ball-in-the-hole games."

Ballsaway was a plastic-covered, flat box whose green inside bottom contained depressions into which the player had to insert small yellow balls by tilting the box this way and that.

Saying he'd had one as a child, Yobo bought a Ballsaway game, and they moved on to the next booth—a game called "Blowemup Military Holomap." A fat little actor was explaining it to a skimpy audience.

"The court jester has told us that other worlds have real, not imagined, military forces. In this game you mark military positions on a mythical world called Terra Firma. For each enemy force blown up, players get ten credits for paying spies and advancing strategic positions on the map . . ."

"Bah!" said Yobo, marching on after only a glance. "More of Ing's dirty work. He's teaching Izz to be just like Earth, reveling in power, paranoia, and mayhem."

—Jeff, don't tell the admiral, but one of the enemy figures in that game looked remarkably like him.

—There's Xeena. Wow, but she's beautiful.

—Jeff! Get a grip on your emotions!

Jeff dragged Norby after Yobo, who was already in the next demonstration area. Xeena was speaking in her melodious voice.

"Take a Teenytrip, citizens. The device can be used in two

ways. First, as a conventional feely, in which you seem to be participating in what you see on the holov screen, your favorite recorded story of villains and heros and lovers"—Xeena smiled shyly—"or anything that's being broadcast at the moment. You can be part of a sports event, or even feel as if you are actually in Izzhall tomorrow for Affirmation Day."

"So what's teeny about those trips?" asked a raucous boy.

"Nothing," said Xeena. "Teenytrip is named for the second way it can be used—to explore the subatomic universe. Once connected to your holov set, Teenytrip gives you so many sensational experiences that you won't want to play with any other computer game. Buy it now!"

And they did. Those who had already bought and used it seemed to come back to share enthusiasm with those just buying it, or perhaps to look at Xeena again.

"I could have invented that," Norby said, "and made lots of money."

"A feely game?" Yobo said sarcastically. "Ing didn't invent that either. Virtual reality experiences via holov have been around the Federation for a long time."

He was close enough to Xeena for her to hear him. She came over and presented him with a game. "Dear Admiral of the amazing head, please try a Teenytrip. Ing will be so pleased."

"I don't give a hoot about pleasing Ing."

Xeena's full lower lip trembled, and she whispered, "Please try the game. I don't care about enriching Ing, but this is my job and I don't want to seem like a failure."

"Oh, okay." Yobo sat down at one of the computer terminals and inserted the small oblong plate that was in the Teenytrip box. He put a connector band around his head and turned on the holov.

To Jeff, watching, the holoscreen showed a primitive version of an old Earth Virtual Reality game called "Acrobatics." Yobo was obviously unimpressed, for he switched to one of the live channels from the holov station. In a comfortable living-room scene Ing was singing a commercial about fruit-and-nut bread.

Yobo grunted. "Adequate virtual reality. I feel as if I'm sitting next to that glowing fireplace, I can reach out and taste the bread—highly spiced, not bad—and Ing seems so three dimensional that I can almost smell him. Xeena, how do I get to the teeny part of the trip?"

"You press that switch."

Yobo did so, and instantly Jeff saw on the screen shifting patterns, colored nebulosities, and weird sparks. Even in holov, without the virtual reality connection, the scene was fascinating and made him want to try the game himself.

Yobo had shut his eyes.

"Admiral," said Norby, "you're not looking at the screen."

"I don't have to. My mind sees where I am."

"Where are you?" asked Jeff.

"In the fields of reality, Cadet. Now don't bother me. I'm studying change."

Jeff stood, shifting his weight from one foot to another, waiting for the admiral to finish. All the other terminals were occupied, and Xeena had left, so he couldn't ask her to get him a terminal and a game.

Norby tugged at Jeff's sleeve. "This is boring, and we're not finding Pera. I want to go outside and cruise the traffic lanes. If I circle slowly around Izzcapital—even the whole continent—I might be able to get a glimmer of Pera's energy patterns."

"Maybe there's nothing wrong after all, and Pera's already gone back to the princess. Maybe she's lost her small tele-pathic ability, and you imagined hearing her cry for help."

"I didn't imagine it!"

Before Jeff could go on arguing, the crowd in Izzhall began to clap. Everyone was looking up, so Jeff raised his eyes to the high domed ceiling. As he watched, it changed from

40

translucent to transparent. He was not sure it opened anywhere, yet hundreds of balloons suddenly appeared as if by magic. The crowd began to yell.

"Ing! Ing! Ing!"

At the very top, one bright red balloon expanded until it seemed certain to burst. There was a flash of light like a miniature lightning bolt from the balloon to the stage, which instantly rose to meet the descending balloon.

The balloon burst in a thunderclap, and there on the stage stood the fair's master of ceremonies, the spangles on his clothing glittering through a gauzy red cape he'd wrapped around himself. He held a small drum and, with a gesture, caused a trapdoor to open, letting up the singers.

"Izzian comrades!" Ing said, obviously into a body mike. "It's showtime! And here's the fairest flower of Izz—Xeena, in a—sob—love duet with my rival, Garus."

Everyone laughed as Ing beat a mournful tattoo upon the drum and then sat crosslegged to provide the percussion to Garus's music. Xeena and Garus began to sing.

"Admiral!" Jeff whispered in his ear, "the show's begun."

Yobo paid no attention. His eyes looked glazed.

Norby touched the admiral and then said, "Jeff, he's in some sort of trance. I can't even reach him telepathically."

"Pull out the plug, Norby."

Norby fiddled with the computer terminal and suddenly the holoscreen went blank. The admiral yawned and stretched as if he had just awakened. At the other terminals Izzians continued to watch the Teenytrip game, as if no show were going on.

"Lover, do not leave me . . ." Garus sang, while Xeena warbled an obbligato: "Let's see who is next on my list . . ."

And at that moment, someone screamed. Towering over everyone, the guard robots were advancing into Izzhall. Crowds parted before them like herd animals escaping

41

predators. The guards seemed to be trying to catch some-thing small and low down. Jeff couldn't see what it was, but he heard an incredible noise.

It sounded like a great, enraged beast.

7.

Cultural Clash

Suddenly the invaders were visible. Scrambling up onto the stage were living Jylots, angrily shaking their tentacles and emitting a noise that started like a lion's roar and ended with a trumpet scream like a furious elephant's.

Ing stood up, clutching his drum, while Garus put his arm around Xeena and moved to the back of the stage. The largest Jylot, whose hide was a darker blue than the rest, waddled up to Ing. Its eyes seemed to shoot out of its bulbous head; then Jeff realized that they were on extensible stalks. It was also obvious that actual Jylots, however blue all over, were minus any hair above their tentacles.

"We, the Jylot, are the native species of Izz and we demand to be treated with proper respect!"

A small boy in the front row of spectators yelled: "I give it back!" and threw a Jylot doll at the Jylot leader.

As the Jylot picked up the doll, Ing cleared his throat. "Hey, listen, nobody meant disrespect. Kids love the doll, and they'll love you if you behave yourselves . . ."

"You have direly insulted our species. Our culture."

"Who, me?"

"Yes, you. We have made inquiries. We know that the outrage is your fault, Ing. You are court scientist and the main inventor on Izz."

Ing gulped. "But I didn't intend—that is, we're just promoting appreciation of your species. After all, Izzians—I mean Izzian humans—have given you sovereignty of your own islands—why, comet tails! You guys . . ."

"We are hermaphroditic, but consider ourselves female."

43

"Um, yes. As I was saying, centuries ago you gals said no humans were allowed to fish near or walk on your islands, so they don't. They trade goods for your sea food and sea jewels. Just because a cute little toy . . ."

"It is not cute! It is sacrilegious!"

Ing plucked the doll from the Jylot leader, who instantly grabbed it back.

"We will take six cases of these dolls . . ."

"Take them all. Dump them in the sea. I don't care."

"Why should we dump them in the sea? They *are* cute."

Ing stared down at the Jylot. "What are we talking about, ma'am?"

"My name is Blawf. I am leader of the Jylots. As long as we're here at the fair, we'll order some dolls for our young ones, but you must destroy all examples of Ballsaway or we'll go on strike, and you humans will have no more sea produce."

"Ballsaway! It's just a little game! What is wrong with it?" Ing whined.

"We hold sacred the shape of the ball . . ."

"To represent the sun?"

"No. The star that shines on Izz may be round—you humans keep saying it is not a flat disc—but the ball that we hold sacred is the egg."

"Wait a minute," Ing interrupted, "eggs aren't round."

"Ours are. It is sacrilege to put into a silly game the magnificent Order and Majesty of Procreation."

Jeff almost laughed until he realized that Izzhall had become terribly silent. Ing was raising his eyebrows, with an amused quirk to his mouth, but the Izzian humans seemed shocked, for their culture was more puritanical than Earth's.

"Order and Majesty?" Ing asked in a strangled voice.

"Of Procreation," Blawf said sonorously, all her tentacles waving rhythmically.

"But human toys and games are full of ball shapes . . ."

"We object only to the game Ballsaway, for we Jylot produce beautiful yellow eggs, which we place in certain green sea plants growing along our island shores. This hideous game permits humans to juggle our eggs until they fill the green holes. We will not stand for such blasphemy . . ."

"Gimme that." Ing bent down and snatched a Ballsaway game from a nearby Izzian, who was holding it out as if it might explode at any moment. "I didn't program the manufacturer's computer with those colors. The background's supposed to be black to make it harder to see the holes, and the balls are supposed to be silver. I had a game like that as a kid . . ."

"Ah, then you didn't invent it," Garus said sardonically.

"Well, no," said Ing. "Who reprogrammed the factory?"

"No one will believe you didn't," said Garus, turning to Blawf. "I am the queen's relative, and I think I can speak for her at this time. Perhaps the game manufacturer . . ."

"Right here," said a stubby man who was sweating a good deal. "I swear the programming wasn't for yellow and green!"

". . . would consider a simple, effective change? Recall all the Ballsaway games and repaint them, using a black background and silver balls."

The Jylots whispered among themselves, and finally Blawf said, "That will be satisfactory."

"Then enjoy the fair, visiting Jylots," said Garus, strumming his instrument and beginning to sing:

> "The sun whose rays are all ablaze,
>   With ever-living glory,
>   Does not deny her majesty . . ."

"That's my song," said Ing, "and you're singing it wrong."

"It's a Gilbert and Sullivan song!" yelled Jeff.

"Shut up, Ing," Garus said, singing on while the Jylots hopped off the stage to mingle with the toy fair crowd.

Jeff saw that the admiral had missed the whole thing. He

had plugged his Teenytrip game into another outlet and sat glued to it.

"Norby, pry the admiral loose again."

Norby's arm extended its full length and he turned off Yobo's computer terminal. The admiral turned to look at them as if he were dazed.

"What was it like, Admiral?"

"There'll be changes. Good changes."

On the stage, Garus sang while Ing grumpily banged the drum and Xeena played a tiny flute.

> "I mean to rule our Izz,
>   as he the sky—
>   We really know our biz,
>   The sun and I!"

Ignoring what Jeff considered to be a significant song, Yobo rose and stretched. "Well, Cadet, I seem to be quite hungry. Where can we have lunch?"

Norby touched Jeff. —Better get him back in the ship. He doesn't look right. It also might be best if I scan for Pera from the ship.

—Okay, but this time we'll stick to the traffic patterns.

Something tugged at the back of Jeff's tunic. He looked around and then down, for it was a Jylot. "Are you Blawf?"

"I am, sir human . . ."

"My name is Jeff. This is my robot Norby, and this is Admiral Boris Yobo. Admiral, the Jylot live on islands . . ."

"Yobo," interrupted Blawf. "A euphonious name, suitable for a unique individual who is the human epitome of mon-umentality and grandeur."

"I am?" asked Yobo, looking more awake.

"I saw you from the stage. I seek your acquaintance. You are the only human I can trust. I am worried about some things we Jylot have discovered, and I would take the prob-

46

lem to the queen, but she has so much hair. They all have so much hair, including you, human Jeff."

"I don't," said Norby. "Can you trust me?"

"You are not organic. But Boris Yobo, sir, you are both organic and, except for a super-oral fringe, without hair on your head. May I join you for the lunch you spoke of?"

"Certainly, Blawf. I am honored."

"We're going to the ship for lunch," Norby said firmly, leading Yobo by the hand.

Yobo insisted on taking the Teenytrip game with him.

In the ship, Jeff, Yobo, and Blawf ate synthesized tuna sandwiches, which Blawf said were delicious. "Someday I should like to visit your Earth, if the seafood is that good."

"I hope you will. Don't you agree, Admiral?" Jeff asked deliberately, hoping to rouse Yobo from his strangely weak, lethargic state. Yobo acted as if he didn't care what happened, as if the only important thing was to wait. And all Yobo would say when asked, "Waiting for what?" was "Change."

And there was the problem of Blawf's tremendous crush on Yobo. Blawf wanted to go along when Yobo went to his cabin for an afternoon nap. Yobo yawned and gave permission, as if it didn't matter. When they disappeared, Norby looked at Jeff.

"How are we going to snap the admiral out of this daze?"

"We ought to find out what the Teenytrip game did."

"I'll investigate it," said Norby. "I don't want you to end up like the admiral." He inserted the game into the ship's computer and turned it to the second mode, the one that had gripped Yobo so. After a few minutes he disconnected.

"It's an excellent VR game, highly imaginative of course, because Ing's never been on a subatomic level, but I can't find anything in it that would upset a human's outlook on life."

"Let me try," said Jeff.

"But . . ."

"You just said it wouldn't hurt. Something else must have happened to the admiral, or there's a subliminal message that only humans can perceive. I have to try to find it. Norby, you take the ship into the traffic patterns over Izzcapital and look for Pera."

The ship rose and began making wider and wider circles while Jeff plugged into the ship's computer and the installed Teenytrip. He tried the first mode and enjoyed a few minutes of a hackneyed old game of trying to beat monster villains who were laying siege to a starbase. To his delight he discovered that with the headband on he could mentally change the appearance of the characters and then, if he concentrated hard enough, the plot. But eventually it bored him and he switched to the second mode.

He was somewhere he'd never been, unable to see clearly what was around him, although he was aware that there were patterns that varied from almost solid to almost ethereal, from incredible colors to a gray that was like the nothingness of hyperspace. His other senses told him more, but it was impossible to put into words.

He *felt* his way through the micro-universe he now seemed to inhabit, not with touch or with emotion, but as if he had extra senses that permitted him an experience beyond reality.

Reality? The real world of Jefferson Wells, ordinary human, sized about halfway between the dimensions of an atom and those of a star? Were humans able to study both atoms and stars because of this coincidence?

Or was reality actually the unified field? And what was a unified field anyway—the groundwork of the universe? Or of the subatomic dimension? Or were they the same thing?

Jeff stopped thinking and just experienced.

"Jeff! Come out of it! Jeff!" Norby was shaking him.

"I'm okay. Connect to the computer. It's quite a game."

"I can sense what you're sensing just by touching you. I think we're way below the level of atoms. Maybe below the quarks and bosons and leptons that make up the universe. This is basically a mess of organized and unorganized energy shapes, probability fields that to us are unpredictable . . ."

"And glorious. It feels as if they must be predictable, except that we don't know how, and the game lets us play in and around the energy shapes. It's like a dance we don't yet understand. Is it a dance of particles? Or are the particles really just dancing probability fields—am I going crazy, Norby? Am I getting like the admiral?"

"You're excited, and I think you could get addicted to a game like this, but"— Norby pulled Jeff's head around and looked into his eyes—"you don't seem drugged. Not like Yobo. And neither of us is talking about change."

"Someone else is here!" Jeff shouted, disconnecting. He discovered that Blawf was standing next to him, tapping Jeff's leg with a tentacle.

"How odd," said Blawf. "I tried to get your attention and found that I was inside the Teenytrip game with you and Norby."

"That's because Jeff and I are telepathic—at least I am, sort of. Jeff is when there's physical contact."

"What's the matter, Blawf?" Jeff asked, for each little blue eye looked ready to cry.

"The wonderful admiral won't listen to me. He yawned when I tried to tell him about our worries, and now he's asleep."

"Not like Yobo," said Norby. "The game affected him in a bad way."

"I have tried that game," said Blawf. "A sailor from one of the freighters that brings goods for barter to our islands gave us a Teenytrip game."

"But how do you play?" asked Jeff. "We were told that there were no electrical wires between Wildpark and the continent."

"Our holovision is beamed from solar satellites," said Blawf. "But I was trying to tell the admiral that I think there *are* wires from Izzcontinent to Wildpark. Jylot deep-water fishers found a line carrying eerie vibrations between Wildpark and the continent. The line crosses some of our best shell gardens. We do not know if this is dangerous."

Norby went back to the ship's control board, which he'd put on autopilot. "I couldn't make contact with Pera here. We might as well investigate what Blawf's told us."

The *Pride* turned and rose above the traffic lanes, then shot toward the seacoast, a kilometer from Izzcapital. Norby took the ship in zigzags from the coast toward the island of Wildpark, a green oval in the blue sea.

Norby said, "You're right, Blawf. There are two kinds of vibrations down there in a straight line from Wildpark. One is a barely perceptible, only occasional vibration of the sea floor. The other is a continuous, powerful electrical transmission. Wildpark is certainly connected electrically to the mainland!"

8.

Wildpark

"I told you there's something evil down there," said Blawf. "What are you going to do about it?"

"In the first place," said Norby, "Jeff and I and the admiral are just visiting, and looking for a lost robot. You should be taking your complaints to the Queen of Izz."

"I've seen her on holov. She scares me."

"And in the second place, electricity isn't necessarily evil. I myself"— Norby placed a two-way hand proudly on his silvery barrel—"function electronically, to the general satisfaction of all concerned."

"But the human Izzians seem to be having some trouble with their highly technological civilization," said Blawf. "Use of machines—even you, Norby—can have dire consequences. Humans should restrict themselves to a primitive life of fishing, farming, and judicious devotion to the Order and Majesty of Procreation."

Jeff smiled. "Tell me, Blawf, would you Jylot really like to give up watching holov? It depends on advanced technology."

The little Jylot was silent for a moment, her tentacles tight against her blue body, her eyestalks completely retracted so that six small blue eyes seemed to be embedded in her head.

Blawf's sigh had a ghost of a whistle at the end of it. "I understand. It is unfortunate, but we do enjoy watching holov. Many of us are fans of the court jester, although I think his hair is too long. The only human whose appearance appeals to me is your admiral. What is wrong with him?"

51

"He watched a Teenytrip game at the fair," said Jeff, "and since then he's acted like a zombie."

"A what?"

"I mean, he acts drugged, lethargic. Like some Izzians we met, his mind seems preoccupied with the concept of change."

"You watched it too," said Blawf. "Are you different?"

"No, Jeff's not," said Norby. "I could tell if he were."

"We should investigate the vibrations down there," said Jeff. "Shall we take you home first, Blawf? I'd love to see your island."

"I'm sorry, but ordinarily our islands are forbidden to non-Jylots. In the Legends of Izz the Others restricted the human settlers to Izzcontinent and Wildpark, and humans have obeyed, keeping their population at a level where they would not need to colonize our islands. All was in harmony until we learned of the Ballsaway game, which we have now dealt with. As Jylot leader, I must find out if the new vibrations from Wildpark are dangerous to us. I want to go with you."

"Down we go," said Norby.

As the *Pride* descended, Jeff's spirits rose, for the large island of Wildpark was remarkably beautiful, a green gem that resolved into a cluster of hills covered by thick forest, surrounded by beaches of golden sand.

The big landing field–parking lot was empty. Blawf said that tourists from all over the continent were not going to spend money going to Wildpark during the famous toy and game fair week. Norby landed gently, but Yobo's senses were not too drugged to miss the change in the ship when the engines stopped. He woke up and wandered in.

"Hello, Admiral," Jeff said nervously, afraid Yobo would be annoyed at their presumption in setting the ship's destination. "This is Wildpark. We're going to visit Garus's father, the park ranger."

"That's nice," said Yobo, yawning at the viewscreen. "Nice place. Be a nice visit, waiting for change."

"What change, Admiral?"

Yobo blinked. "The change. Expected. Tomorrow, I think. All us Izzians will back it up."

"Admiral, you're not an Izzian."

Yobo blinked again. "No?" He yawned again. "Doesn't matter. Let's get some food and play the game some more."

They left the ship and headed for a rustic lodge made of unpainted wood weathered to soft gray. The Izzian version of rocking chairs filled the wide porch, which was surrounded by bright flowers. A man sat in one of the rockers, moving gently back and forth, his wide hat tilted back on his red hair.

"Greetings," the man said, rising. "I'm Ranger Orran. My wife has taken our flitter to Izzcapital, to see the last day of the toy fair, but I'll be happy to take care of you visitors. We have a great robot chef, and until after the Affirmation ceremonies, we've no other guests."

Yobo yawned and sat heavily in a rocker. "Do you have a holov set? To watch the change."

"What change?" Orran's freckled forehead wrinkled.

"Why—*the* change. We must wait, and then approve." Yobo smiled vaguely at Orran and closed his eyes.

"Ranger, I'm Jeff Wells, that's Admiral Boris Yobo, and this is my robot Norby. We're visitors from off the planet, and Blawf is showing us around."

"Blawf, eh? Heard of you, I have. Head of the Jylot."

Surreptitiously, Jeff examined his stock of credits. "We can't afford to stay at the lodge for the night. We'll have to stay in our ship, but we'd like to eat here. Is that okay?"

"Certainly. Welcome to Wildpark lodge."

Norby said, "Where's the big machine that has a cable going from here to Izzcontinent?"

"What machine?" asked Orran.

"On our way here we thought we detected some electrical vibrations underwater," said Jeff.

"Impossible," said Orran. "Wildpark is cut off from Izz-continent except by satellite holov."

Jeff touched Norby's hat. —He seems innocent.

—He's Garus's father, and you heard Garus sing about wanting to rule Izz.

—That's only a song. But I suppose you're right, Norby. Maybe we'd better not explain anything yet.

—I agree. [That was Blawf, tuning in with one of her tentacles touching Norby.]

"Had lunch?" asked Orran.

"I think the admiral is still hungry," said Jeff, but Yobo started snoring. "Perhaps when he wakes up you and your robots can give him afternoon tea. We'll try to be back for it, but right now we'd like to take a walk in the woods."

"Go right ahead, young feller. I'll just sit here and rock until your hairless friend wakes up. The hiking trail starts over there."

The paths were lined with soft pieces of bark, bordered by ferns, and shaded by immense trees that could only have come from primeval temperate forests of Earth. Birds abounded, small animals scurried, and Jeff glimpsed deer moving sedately and unafraid in the distance.

They walked on until the path narrowed to go between two high outcrops of irregular stone. Norby stopped.

"Scanning, Norby?"

"Trying to. It's very difficult. There's something big here on Wildpark. Big, inorganic, and possibly sentient, although I'm not sure. Whatever it is doesn't seem aware of us, and for all I know, it isn't truly conscious. But there's mental power, and lots of electrical power. I just can't focus in on it. There seems to be an odd force-field shielding it."

"Then you can't go into hyperspace and out again to where this thing is?"

"I don't think so, but I have an idea. Blawf, Jeff and I have to leave for a while . . ."

"No! Take me with you!"

"You can go back to the lodge to be with the admiral."

"You're going investigating, and as leader of the Jylot I must go along. If there's something wrong with Wildpark, it may affect the Jylot islands, so I must find out. Besides, we've walked quite a ways, and to get back to the lodge I may be set upon by wild land animals. I am primarily a creature of sea and shore, and do not run fast on land."

"I'll carry you, Blawf," Jeff said, picking her up. She put two tentacles around his neck so it was easy to carry her with one arm and give his other hand to Norby.

"We're going into hyperspace, Blawf," said Norby. "Humans say that's the nothingness of everything, but they don't know what that means and neither do I. It will seem gray and odd to you, but you'll be able to breathe in my air-bubble for the time it takes me to travel back."

"Back where?"

Norby didn't answer her. They entered hyperspace and Jeff felt Blawf tremble, but she didn't cry out.

—Where are we going, Norby?

—To see the beginning, Jeff.

They seemed to pop out of the gray of hyperspace and immediately sunlight beat down upon Jeff, forcing him to shut his eyes until he could adapt. When he opened them, the left-hand rock looked exactly the same, but there were no trees anywhere and the right-hand rock was missing. In its place was a huge hole, with metal steps going down into the ground.

"Ships," Norby said softly. "In orbit. You can't see them, but I can sense them. Very big ships, not Izzian, and not Terran."

"Where are we?" asked Blawf.

"Same place, different time," said Norby, walking to the steps. "Before Izz was terraformed to be more like Earth."

"But somebody's here," Jeff said, "from the ships. Busy digging holes in the ground and building a staircase, I suppose in case the power fails and lifts won't work. Have the Others built this—and if so, why did they hide it? I didn't see anything like it on the Wildpark of our day—if this is truly still Wildpark."

"No plants," Blawf said mournfully. "No animals. And this is the island that will become Wildpark, for you can see my island just over there, and the other Jylot islands. In the distance you can see Izzcontinent. But even my island has no vegetation. Where are my ancestors?"

"I don't know, Blawf," said Norby. "Maybe they're still in the sea and haven't evolved to be able to walk on land."

Jeff said, "But the Others put paleolithic humans on Izz. There wouldn't be enough time from then until our day for the Jylot to evolve into land-dwelling animals."

"Oh dear!" Blawf wailed. "Where are my ancestors?"

Norby teetered on the top step. "I suggest that we stop speculating and investigate this time we're now in, because there's a big machine at the bottom of these steps." His metal feet clattered going down the metal stair rungs.

Jeff followed, carrying Blawf because the Jylot's short legs didn't work well on steps. The light was only a dim glow from the walls. They went down and down, around and around the spiral staircase, until the air was as cool as a cave.

The bottom *was* a cave. Before Jeff could see anything else, a big, silent robot loomed up, grabbed him, and set off an alarm that echoed like a hollow voice of doom.

Interlopers

"Let go of Jeff, you big lummox!" Norby shouted, tugging at the robot's arm.

"It's not hurting me," Jeff said, one arm aroud Blawf and the other in the grasp of the robot, which looked exactly like the big Izzian guard robots. "Are you arresting me, guard?"

The robot said nothing, and seemed to be waiting.

"What's that thing?" Blawf asked, pointing a tentacle.

Peering into the semi-darkness, Jeff saw an enormous metal box with strange dials and pressure switches along one side.

"It's a computer," Norby said. "Unshielded. I could fiddle with it . . ."

"No!" Jeff shouted. "Don't touch it! Not only is this robot now aiming a gun at you, but if you do anything to change the past . . ."

"Okay, okay. I was just tempted. In our day the Others have fancier computers, but I'm sure it's one of theirs."

Jeff tried to wriggle out of the robot's grasp, but it held tightly. "Norby, take Blawf back to our time so she'll be safe. Then come back here with help. Maybe the ranger has a gun that will stun this robot long enough for me to get loose."

"I will stay with you, Jeff," Blawf said. "You are hairy, but I like you."

"You two organics must go back to our own time. There's nothing for you to eat on the planet now," said Norby.

"I will fish for food," Blawf said, patting Jeff's cheek. "I will feed you."

"Someone's coming," Norby said, hovering on antigrav

between Jeff and the mammoth computer. "A door just opened."

Indeed, Jeff felt a current of air start, and then he heard quiet footsteps. His heart thumping, he saw a darker shadow round the corner of the computer.

Emerging into the dim light of the cave, the stranger proved to be a medium-sized Other, hairless—and therefore male—and carrying a box of tools with his lower pair of arms. The upper arms were folded across his slim chest. His three eyes stared at Jeff in obvious astonishment.

"Hello, sir," Jeff said in Izzian, remembering that it was the Others who had taught that language to the human settlers.

"You are human," the Other said, using the Izzian term.

"Yes, sir. I'm Jeff Wells. This is Blawf, a Jylot, and my robot, Norby. Could you ask your robot to release me? I don't intend any harm. We saw the staircase and were curious."

The Other put down the toolbox and folded both pairs of arms. "In our ships we have many humans, collected from all over the planet Earth. They are being held in stasis until this planet of Izz has been terraformed for them. These humans are not civilized. They do not have the technology to make clothes like yours and certainly not a robot like yours. You can only be from the future."

"Yes, sir," Norby said, blinking in agitation. "Nobody can time travel except me, so don't worry about that. As for why we're here, it's an awfully long story . . ."

"I do not want to hear the story. Nothing must be changed now that would alter the future. Knowledge imparted to me may do just that."

"Could we ask you a question, sir?" Jeff was suddenly released, for the Other had motioned to the big robot.

"I will see whether it is safe to answer you. Go ahead."

"That huge computer over there. Is it like the one that's sealed up on Izzcontinent?"

"Your question implies that in your time, there has been no need to use this computer. I am not a computer expert, but I have seen Mainbrain One, on the continent, and this Mainbrain Two, buried beneath the largest island, which will become a nature sanctuary. Both computers look the same to me."

Norby said, "Why have you Others installed two computers on the planet, and is there a connection between them?"

"Electrical cables go in a tunnel from Mainbrain One to this Mainbrain Two. We have given this world two Mainbrains to be fail-safe. Do you know this principle?"

"Yes, sir. Will both computers be activated?"

"No, small robot. Only Mainbrain One." The Other shook his smooth head. "I am worried about talking to you. I wish my father were here. Perhaps I had better consult with him before I ask you questions about the future. My father always says that my curiosity causes trouble."

Jeff grinned, for he suddenly realized that this Other was perhaps almost as young as he. "Where's your father?"

"He is in the lead ship, in charge of this transplanting expedition. We have finished putting in machinery, and the next stage is the planting. I came back to get the toolbox I negligently left behind." The Other grinned, too. "I wish I could get to know you humans better. You are not a bad sort when you are civilized and speak our language."

Jeff said, "I have always wondered why the Others brought humans from Earth to settle on Izz."

"Father says that humans are the sentient species that will come to dominate their home planet. We Others have had experience with various sentient species in different parts of the universe. Once they develop a technological civilization, many of these species destroy themselves and their planets."

"Humans almost did . . ." Norby began.

"Shut up," Jeff said. "But why Izz?"

"Father says Earth is so beautiful that my species wished to create another Earth in case anything goes wrong with

59

the original. This planet we have called Izz does not measure up to the variety of beauty on Earth, but it is a good planet, and will be a haven for the human species, as well as for the many animals and plants we are moving here."

"Please tell your father that we are grateful," said Jeff. "Norby, I think we'd better go back to our own time."

"Wait!" yelled Blawf. "What about *my* species? Where are my ancestors, native to this planet?"

"There are no creatures like you on the planet, but Father has been talking about rescuing the remnants of a species left on another planet we recently discovered, one whose sun is dying. I think they look like you. They are biochemically similar to Earth creatures, so they might be able to succeed living here on Izz."

"Ah," said Blawf. "Then we Jylot are also immigrants, displaced beings. How will I ever be able to tell my relatives that we are not the proud natives of Izz?"

Jeff hugged the little Jylot. "Blawf, you can be proud of being survivors and managing to live so successfully on a strange planet, with difficult creatures like human beings for neighbors."

"I suppose so. Perhaps it is not a disgrace."

Norby walked up to the Other. "We need a little more help. We have to know how to get into the computer chambers. Is there a special password or something?"

"Open sesame?" muttered Jeff.

"Then there is trouble in the future—no, don't tell me. I shouldn't have talked to you at all. I've pressed the emergency call switch on my belt and Father will come soon. He will no doubt be very annoyed with you—and with me."

"Please," Norby said, "what's the password?"

"No words, only a special key, to be given to the ruler of Izz. Has it been lost?"

"I don't know." Norby shuffled his two-way feet. "We might need to use it, soon. I suspect the queen won't give it to us, so we might have to steal it, except that it would help if we knew what it looked like."

"Father does not approve of stealing."

"Neither do we," Jeff said hurriedly, "but we're sort of having an emergency up in our own time. Please, couldn't you explain to your father . . ."

"I do not think so. My father is a very strict being, and I do tend to get into trouble." The Other laughed. "Oh, well, why not? This is the best adventure I have ever had, meeting you from the future. The key is thin, round, pointed at one end, and incised with a pattern the computers and the door locks can read."

"Thank you," Jeff said. "We'd better not endanger the future—our time—by staying any longer. Goodbye. I hope you enjoy the rest of your life."

There was a strange sound, like tiny bells tinkling very rapidly. Blawf shrieked, "What's that!"

"Father has beamed to the surface. He'll come down the steps any moment. Maybe you had better run into the tunnel and go to your own time from there. Goodbye."

"Goodbye!" Norby said, grabbing the hand Jeff wasn't using to hold Blawf and lifting both of them into the air. He hurtled around the corner of the big computer and through an open door into a large tunnel, whose ceiling bore an obviously new cable.

The tunnel seemed to shudder into gray nothingness for a moment, and then there was a sickening lurch that almost made Jeff lose his skimpy lunch. They were still in the tunnel.

"What's wrong, Norby? Can't we get to our own time?"

"We are in our time. See, the door's shut." Norby deposited Jeff on the dusty tunnel floor and flew to the door. "It's also locked and I can't open it. We can't return to the surface this way, although I suppose if I went back into hyperspace and maneuvered a bit I might be able to get into normal space on the surface of the planet."

"Or in solid rock. No thanks." Jeff looked around and saw that the tunnel was not the same. Large, shining rails were fixed to the bottom, one at each side. Overhead the cable looked dusty and old. "Norby, take us to the other end of the tunnel, and I think we'll emerge into Izzhall. Maybe we'll also find out who's been down here, for someone has. There aren't any footprints, but there's a dusted space just in front of the door, between the two rails. Someone walked on the rails, cleared the space, and probably opened the door with the key."

Blawf said, "The ceiling cable now emanates the same continuous vibrations that we Jylot started to feel on the sea floor, starting less than a year ago."

"Because Mainbrain Two is operating now," said Norby. "I could sense it through the locked door. Ing must have the key. Come on, we'll see if the other end of the tunnel is open."

Norby sped them through the tunnel until it ended at an identical door. There was a difference, however, for at the end of each rail was a monocar big enough to carry four people, two in front and two in back, or lots of cargo.

"These conveyances must be what makes the discontinuous vibration we Jylot have felt."

Norby touched the door's surface. "Same strange lock that I can't open. See, there's a small, round opening . . ."

"For a thin, long key," Jeff finished. "The space before this door is also dusted, with no footprints. And the carriages have been dusted. I wish we had a fingerprint kit."

"We can't go around fingerprinting everyone on Izz," said Norby. "But you're right—get fingerprints from here, and then go back to Earth and compare them with Ing's prints— what am I saying? All I have to do is scan the prints, and then shake hands with Ing here on Izz!"

Norby's sensor wire went out full length, moving over the carriages. When he'd scanned both, he said, "Sorry. Good idea, but no fingerprints. Whoever uses these carriages uses gloves. Nobody on Izz would be sophisticated enough to do that except Ing."

"But if Ing has the key, where is it?" asked Jeff.

Blawf tapped Jeff with a tentacle. "I took a good look at the master of ceremonies when I confronted him about the sacrilegious Ballsaway game. He's got so many gold spangles on his clothes; perhaps he's hidden the key among them?"

Norby and Jeff looked at each other.

"If Ing has the key, the mystery is how he got it," said Norby. "It belongs to the ruler of Izz. Surely the queen didn't give it to him."

"The royal family may have long forgotten the purpose of the key," Jeff said. "Ing's a computer expert, so perhaps he saw the key and recognized that the markings could be computer instructions, a way of opening up the doors and the Mainbrain itself."

"Two Mainbrains, since they're both operating now," said Norby. "I don't know why he's using both. Perhaps we should go back to talk to the young Other's father, and find out if the Mainbrains function differently."

"No!" Jeff said. "We mustn't meddle in the past."

"And besides," Blawf said, "I don't want to meet an angry father and leader of an expedition, although I suppose I should be grateful to them for rescuing my species."

Jeff shifted Blawf to his other arm and took Norby's hand again. "Get a good fix on that door, Norby. On the other side is Mainbrain One. Perhaps you can go into hyperspace and out again on the other side of the door. We must find out what Ing's been doing."

"We know what he's been doing," said Norby. "Bollixing up the political and economical structure of Izz so he can take over. An ingenious plan, scheduled to come to fruition tomorrow on Affirmation Day. We must stop him, Jeff. I'll just get on the other side of the door . . ."

The quick dip into hyperspace was over almost before it

registered on Jeff, and then he was aware that he'd landed hard on the seat of his pants, with bright lights shining.

It seemed as if hundreds of people were staring at him. He blinked, and they still were. They began to laugh.

"That's a good trick!" yelled somebody in the crowd.

A musical instrument twanged. Jeff looked back and up at an angry face—Ing's.

> "Citizens, you should beware
> Robots who come out of air—
> Interlopers, begone!
> A curse hereupon
> If you don't exit my fair!"

Ing bent down to hiss in Jeff's ear, "Get out of my act, kid, or I'll tell the guard robots to lock you up!"

10.

Mainbrain

Norby, still holding Jeff, spoke telepathically.

—Oops!

—We're in Izzhall, Norby! Officer Luka is getting out her stun gun in case we're not part of the act. And I can see Garus and Xeena. Garus doesn't look pleased. Why did you bring us here?

—I think I was focusing on Ing, and here we are.

Ing kicked Jeff. "Avast there, me slave. Now that I have summoned you from the realm of magic"—he switched to Terran Basic: "Stand up, you oaf! Dance! Sing! Do something or you'll ruin my act"—Ing laughed fiendishly and continued in Izzian. ". . . you must do as I say. Sing, varlet!"

—Better do it [that was Norby], because Luka suspects us and I see a guard robot on its way.

Jeff stood up, cleared his throat, and struggled to put into Izzian an old Space Academy song.

> "We sail the space lanes wide,
> And our saucy ship's a beauty—
> The Federation's pride—
> We cadets all do our duty."

The audience, more or less mystified, clapped, and Jeff bowed as Ing hissed in his ear again.

"That doesn't go in translation, boy. In fact, your singing stinks. Blast you, Jefferson Wells. No matter where I go in this universe, you always show up to cramp my style."

"Hey, Ing!" shouted someone in the crowd. "The boy's playing with a Jylot doll!"

"So he is. And a toy robot." Ing snatched Blawf from Jeff's arms. "Dolls belong with younger children, or juggling jesters, don't they?"

"Yes!" roared the crowd. "Juggle the Jylot!"

Luka and the guard robot had almost reached the stage, and Jeff could see Garus pushing his way through the crowd while Xeena held back as if frightened.

Ing also picked up a genuine Jylot doll and began to juggle it in tandem with the real Jylot. At first Blawf was as limp as a doll, but suddenly she twisted in the air, landed on Ing's shoulder, and pinched his nose.

"Ow!"

"The hat!" shouted Norby.

Blawf tore off Ing's pointed helmet.

"It's here!" she said, throwing it to Norby.

"Jump!" shouted Jeff, and Blawf hurled herself into Jeff's arms, ripping some of Ing's costume on the way.

"Cursed cadets!" Ing yelled in Terran Basic. "Go home! Get off my planet!" Then he aimed his fist at Jeff's nose.

There was no connection. Jeff's stomach lurched again and by the next blink, his eyes opened in a white room containing a huge metal box with familiar dials and pressure switches.

"Welcome to Mainbrain One," Norby said, letting go of Jeff. "Very efficient of me to think of getting Ing's helmet."

"I suspect that actually you were mixed up, as usual."

"Now, Jeff, maybe I didn't think consciously of going to Ing in order to take the key, but my unconscious . . ."

"Since when do robots have unconscious processes?"

"I probably do. I have emotive circuits. I am a very special robot, with delicate feelings and sensitivity."

"Uh-huh. Well, we're here, with the key, thanks to you, Blawf." Jeff put the little Jylot on the floor and stretched, for his arms were beginning to feel cramped.

Blawf stretched too, all her tentacles flipping out and back rhythmically for a second. "This room is old—see how the walls are covered by fine cracks—but the floor is clean. Do you think Ing dusts it or does someone help him?"

"That's a thought," said Jeff. "Maybe it's a genuine conspiracy aimed at dethroning Queen Tizzle, not just Ing trying to make mischief or promote himself to kingship."

"Silly old megalomaniac Ing." Norby walked over to Mainbrain One. "I'll find out what he's been doing to the computer system." Without first removing the attached helmet, Norby stuck the gold point into a hole he found in the middle of the set of dials on Mainbrain One. After a minute of poking, he tore the court jester's helmet from the gold stick.

"Jeff, this isn't the key to the computer. There are no incised patterns. The surface is perfectly smooth."

"Maybe it only unlocks the door."

Norby went to the door and tried it. "Nope. Doesn't work. I can't open the lock." He walked back to the computer, fiddled with its dials and switches, and finally touched it for several minutes with his sensor wire, his metal eyelids closed.

"What's the matter?" asked Jeff.

Norby opened his eyes. "No matter what I do to this metal monster, it won't respond."

"Monster?" Blawf's voice quavered. "Is it alive?"

Norby said, "I've been wondering if it has the kind of computer brain that is considered to be alive and conscious. I, for instance, am a striking example of this . . ."

"But what about this Mainbrain?" Jeff asked.

"Mainbrain One, like Mainbrain Two, is a very big computer brain, capable of running the entire computer system for this planet. In fact, Mainbrain One's been doing just that ever since the Others set it up back when Earth was in its paleolithic period."

"But is it intelligent? Conscious?"

"That's the strange thing, it isn't, and not because most of it has recently been turned off . . ."

"What!"

"Oh, I haven't mentioned that yet?"

"No, you haven't, Norby."

"Well, remember that the Other told us they weren't going to activate Mainbrain Two? And that when we came to our own time, in the tunnel, Mainbrain Two was turned on?"

"So?"

"I detected that Mainbrain Two is going full blast. I didn't have long to scan it, and I couldn't have entered its programming anyway, but I'm fairly sure that Mainbrain Two, on full, is not a conscious intelligence. It is powerful, but it probably only responds to instructions given it. Same with Mainbrain One."

"But why has Mainbrain One been only partly turned off? Why didn't Ing close it down completely if Mainbrain Two has taken over?"

"I think Mainbrain One's being used as a transmitter for the commands Mainbrain Two sends it through that cable over there, coming from the tunnel. Since the Mainbrain output runs Izz, that means Mainbrain Two is running Izz, through Mainbrain One, which can no longer be used to change the programming."

"I'm not sure I understood all that," Blawf said, each little blue eye blinking, "except that we've brought the wrong key."

Jeff felt tired and discouraged. "I don't understand why Ing would use Mainbrain Two for his evil schemes. The young Other said the two computers were identical, Norby."

"No, he said they looked alike to him. The computer hardware may look the same, but the programming may be different. I'd guess that Ing had to turn off most of Mainbrain One's functions because he can control only Mainbrain Two."

"With what?" asked Blawf.

"We don't know." Norby stuck the gold point back into the court jester's hat. "Certainly not with this."

"The helmet is a decoy," Jeff said, removing the point from the hat and pocketing it. "Ing's hidden the real key somewhere. Maybe it's here."

"If the key is hidden in a locked room, how would Ing get in?" asked Blawf.

"Easy," said Norby. "All he'd have to do is use the right key to get into Mainbrain Two, program it to shut down most of and control the rest of Mainbrain One, and at the same time program the doors to open to him alone."

"You mean that every time he wants to manipulate the computer system he has to take one of those monorail carriages over to Wildpark?"

"No, Jeff. I'd bet that with the right key Ing can control Mainbrain Two from any computer terminal anywhere on the planet. Remember that there's only one computer system, completely integrated."

"In the Federation," Jeff said slowly, "you don't need almost-magical keys to control computers. All you need is the right code signals. Ever since computer systems were invented, people have been breaking into them, sometimes from far away."

"Yes, Jeff, but a one-and-only key, given to the ruling family to be used in secret, is a better way of keeping a computer system out of the hands of wicked hackers."

"Not when the key is stolen by one of them."

Blawf sighed. Jeff sighed. Norby's head descended until only the tops of his eyes showed.

"What do we do now?" asked Blawf.

No one answered her, for at that moment there was an almost imperceptibly faint sound nearby.

Norby's hat shot up, and his legs extended full length. "I've sensed that the doorlock has just been unlocked."

"Which door?" asked Jeff. "There ought to be two—one

69

to the tunnel and one to the corridor under—what are we under?"

"About halfway between the palace and Izzhall," Norby said. "The tunnel door must be hidden by the computer, for the one we're looking at, the one that just unlocked, goes outside, not to the tunnel."

The visible door suddenly slammed into its wall slot, and two large figures stood against the brighter light of the corridor outside.

They stepped quickly into the Mainbrain room and, more quickly, the door shut behind them.

"Guard robots!" Blawf said, scurrying behind the computer.

Norby stood his ground, his small barrel form between Jeff and the advancing robots.

"I'll get you out of here, Jeff. One of them has a gun. These police robots sure distort the laws of robotics."

"What do you want?" Jeff yelled.

The guard to Jeff's right fired at Norby, whose arms and legs and head withdrew into his barrel. As Norby fell on the floor of the computer room, Jeff tried to catch him.

"Do not touch that robot!" said the right-hand guard in a deep, grating voice without any inflections.

"Give me that gun!" Jeff commanded. "I am a human being and my orders take precedence . . ."

The guard fired, and Jeff felt as if the universe were going far away, leaving him in a dark place.

11.

Norby Missing

"Jeff! Human Jeff! Wake up!"

Jeff opened one eye to find another staring into his. The other eye was small, blue, neatly fringed, and seemed to be disembodied. "Blawf—what happened?"

Blawf's eyestalk snapped back into her head and now a ring of blue eyes peered at Jeff. "The talking guard shot you with its gun. The other took Norby inside itself, and both robots left, locking the door to the outside corridor behind them."

Jeff groaned and sat up, feeling as if his head were stuffed full of gravel. "We're trapped. Only Norby can get in and out of locked rooms by going into hyperspace."

"Behind Mainbrain One, the door to the tunnel is unlocked on this side. I would like to venture into the tunnel. Perhaps the door at the other end is now open."

"I think we'd better stay here for a while, in case the robots come back, with Norby."

Blawf's tentacles drooped. "But I am getting thirsty and there's nothing here to drink. Even if there were, it would probably be fresh water, and although we Jylots can drink that, we eventually require ocean water. We imbibe it, bathe in it, perform the Order and Majesty of Procreation in it . . ."

"Okay, Blawf. We'll go to the Mainbrain Two end."

A fast monocar ride took them to the other end of the tunnel, but the door over there was still locked.

"Let's go back to Mainbrain One," Jeff said, suddenly aware that claustrophobia had hit him full force. The dim tunnel seemed like an evil, enclosed space trapping him under unknown kilometers of rock and water that threatened to crush him.

"Jeff, your eyes are fixed in the front of your head and always face the same direction together. My eyestalks can point in several ways at once."

"Yes, Blawf." Jeff felt like screaming, but he tried to be patient. He wanted to get back in the monocar at once, before the sensation of being hopelessly trapped overcame him.

"Well, my upper-pointing eyestalk tells me that there is a small door in the ceiling of the tunnel, perhaps reachable if you stand on the top of the monocar."

She was right. There was indeed a round metal plate in the ceiling, and it had a handle.

"Jeff, if you open it, will the tunnel flood? I can, of course, breathe in water, but I fear you cannot."

"The tunnel won't flood, not if the door works properly. You see, Blawf, it's an airlock, the same sort that the Others use on their ships. At least, I hope it is. I'll let you out, and if you can swim to your island, you'll be safe."

"If you can hold your breath for a few minutes, I will take you to the surface. I think we should both escape, for I doubt if anyone will believe my story."

Jeff looked longingly back through the tunnel toward the Izzcontinent end. It seemed safe back with Mainbrain One, yet he knew it was not. The vicious guard robots could return, and if they did not, he would eventually die of thirst. He climbed on the top of the monocar and found he could reach the handle.

Although the airlock door seemed terribly ancient, and it opened with a groan of its own, the inside was clean and shiny. It had probably never been used since the Others installed it, no doubt as a safety measure. "When I open the outside door, the water will fill the lock. We must wait until it is full before we go out."

"Hold on to this tentacle, Jeff. It's the biggest. And watch out for my feet."

Puzzled, Jeff put the Jylot on the floor of the airlock and held on to her biggest tentacle with his left hand while he manipulated the inside handle with his right hand. At first he thought the lock was rusted shut, for nothing happened.

"Perhaps you have to slide the door aside."

"I think it's blocked by something."

"There is"— the tips of Blawf's remaining tentacles moved over the wall—"a depression here. I will press . . ."

The door suddenly slid back and the ocean descended into the airlock. Frantically, Jeff tried to swim out, but there was a bubble of wire mesh enclosing a small space over the doorway. Jeff was stuck halfway out of the water-filled airlock, wondering which would be worse, to drown or to be cut in half, when the door slid closed again.

Blawf swam into the wire-enclosed space with Jeff clinging to her tentacle, conscious only that the oxygen in his lungs was going. Turning upside down, Blawf stretched the rest of her tentacles to press against the edges of the outer door.

"Boom!" Underwater, Blawf made a noise that sounded like a muffled cannon as her body compressed and then shot backward, her feet against the wires. The mesh bubble seemed to explode, and she turned around, pulling Jeff after her as her feet flapped like a strange propulsion device toward the surface.

He'd forgotten to tell her that humans develop the bends if brought to the surface too quickly, but fortunately, here on the edge of Wildpark Island, the ocean was so shallow that it didn't matter.

Gasping in the air, Jeff was dazzled by the late afternoon sunlight as Blawf towed him toward the shore. When his feet touched the sandy bottom, he took Blawf into his arms and waded ashore on his own power.

"Thanks, Blawf. You've saved us. We'd better go right to the ship. The admiral's been brainwashed by the Teenytrip game, and we can't trust Ranger Orran because he's not only Garus's father, but he's of royal descent and may know about the plot against the present queen."

"That's a good idea, but I don't think it will work."

Squinting up at the shoreline trees, Jeff saw Ranger Orran with a gun pointed down at him. As he watched, the gun lowered.

"Howdy. Fine day for swimming. I wasn't sure what was coming ashore. Your admiral is fit to be tied over your not returning. He wanted to get in the ship and find you, but he's only just come to his senses . . ."

Dripping seawater, Jeff clambered up the bank beside Orran and saw the roof of the Ranger's lodge just beyond the trees. "What do you mean, come to his senses?"

"Well, first he talked constantly about the change, in between his naps. He was angry when he found out we didn't have a Teenytrip game, and couldn't remember what happened to his. He didn't seem to remember that he'd come here by ship, and what with his peculiar behavior, I decided I'd better not tell him the ship was in the parking lot. I didn't know if he'd be fit to pilot it. But after his fourth nap, he seemed to make more sense, and now he's worried about you."

Jeff hurried to the lodge, finding a wide-awake and irate Yobo pacing the porch.

"Where have you been, Cadet? Orran said you went for a walk in the woods. I was sure you were lost, and here I find out you've been swimming . . ."

"Not exactly, Admiral. Are you all right? Thinking about change? Wanting to play the game?"

"Game, game? Oh, that Teenytrip game. Can't remember what we did with it. I suppose it's in the ship. Fun, and full of interesting aspects of change. Or was it questions of change? I can't remember. Odd, when I first got here, I wanted to keep playing the game, but when I realized you were missing, I didn't want to any more. You've come back mighty late for teatime."

"But not too late, I hope," Jeff said. "I'll change clothes in the ship and be right back."

In the ship, he not only showered and put on a fresh outfit, but hid the Teenytrip game so the admiral wouldn't find it. Then he went back to the lodge for what the admiral's Martian family would have called high tea.

Swallowing tea, cake, and tiny fish fritters (which Blawf also enjoyed), Jeff felt enormous relief at knowing the admiral was his old self, listening intently to the description of their adventures. Jeff had told Blawf to focus one eyestalk on Orran's face to see his reaction to what Jeff said.

"I don't understand," Orran said finally. "If your marvelous robot Norby can escape most situations by entering hyperspace or another time, why can't he escape the guard?"

"I think the guard's inside is a stasis chamber, and even Norby can't get out of a stasis chamber by himself."

Orran stroked his chin. "Yes, I remember my grandfather Orz telling me about the special guard robots. It was Orz, you know, who abdicated the kingship in favor of his brother Narrin, the great-grandfather of the present queen. Tizzle and I are about the same age, because when Orz married again, he was elderly. My father was born the same year as Narrin's granddaughter Narriza, mother to Queen Tizzle."

"You're descended from the oldest son," said Yobo. "Don't you think of yourself as the rightful heir to the throne?"

"Not at all. Tizzle's great-grandfather may have been the second son, but after him, her line is completely through females, while mine is through males. She's the rightful ruler of Izz."

"And Garus agrees with that?" asked Jeff.

Orran raised one bushy red eyebrow. "I should think so, but Garus is an actor. I don't understand actors. My father and I wished only to be Wildpark rangers, like Orz. I did not even know that there is another Mainbrain computer buried under Wildpark. I assure you, that is the truth."

Jeff believed him. At least he wanted to believe Orran, because he felt that the more allies he had, the better. Time was running out, for the day was waning and the Affirmation ceremonies would take place tomorrow.

Allies? Jeff was proud of Admiral Yobo, regaining his normal Federation perspective, and of Blawf, the brave Jylot. Orran was almost as big and strong as Yobo, and perhaps as trustworthy. But the villain of Izz had so far been one step ahead of anyone's game.

What can any of us do without Norby? Jeff thought. How can I get him back?

As if he were reading Jeff's mind, Yobo said, "We must rescue Norby, Jeff. We can't go home without him, and much as I like Izz, I prefer my own life in the Federation."

"If there's a mysterious danger to Queen Tizz, I want to help stop it," said Orran. "If you do find your Norby, I hope you'll stay long enough to save the queendom."

"I think we should take the ship back to Izzcapital and tell the queen everything. Maybe she has another key, or can guess who took the original." Jeff sighed. "And if she has ultimate control over all the guard robots, maybe she'll find the one containing Norby."

"Just don't play any Teenytrip games," Blawf said. "We Jylot were not affected, but you humans seem susceptible to a malignant influence from the game. Except Jeff."

Yobo's eyes widened. "Jeff! You tried the game only in the ship! Do you realize what that means?"

"No, sir."

"Blasted Trojan horse, that's what it means."

"I beg your pardon?" said Orran. "What's a Trojan horse?"

Yobo told about Odysseus conquering Troy by filling a wooden horse with soldiers and persuading the Trojans to take it into the city as a gift. "Computers can be programmed with a hidden set of instructions, like the soldiers in the Trojan horse. At a specified time, the effects of these hidden instructions will appear. Ing must have programmed Mainbrain Two to add subliminal messages about change when Teenytrip games are played, making citizens likely to accept the computer's choice of Ing as the rightful ruler on Affirmation Day."

"Could your ex-compatriot, the court jester, accomplish such a feat with computers?" asked Orran.

"He certainly could," said Yobo, "just as he could control those robot guards to take Norby out of the way."

"I understand," said Blawf. "My people, like Jeff, were not affected by the game, because we played it on holov sets unconnected to the main computer system of Izz."

"We must stop Ing, Jeff. We'll take the ship directly to the palace. The queen must be informed."

Jeff began to get suspicious again when Orran said he had to stay on Wildpark, since no one else was there to protect the island, but the ranger seemed genuinely concerned about the threat to the royal family.

His suspicions surfaced again when he, Yobo, and Blawf entered the throne room to find the queen giving audience to Officer Luka, who stood between Ing and Garus, each sporting a black eye. Garus was shouting.

"Cousin Tizz, I protest! I did not hit Ing for nothing. I hit him because he's jealous of me and has abducted Xeena!"

12.

The Queen's Justice

"Garus, you miserable scoundrel!" Ing yelled back. "It's not enough that you try to upstage me all the time, but now you're ruining my act by stealing my soprano! It's a plot! You and Xeena are in cahoots to take over the court jestership. She's probably in your room right now . . ."

"She isn't! She's missing, I tell you, and it's your doing, Ing. You're just pretending outrage. You're an actor, like me, and I know what actors can pretend. It was you who ordered the robot guard to come over when she was singing . . ."

"That was part of the act!" Ing turned to the queen, who was sitting bolt upright on her throne, her face tired. "This is the last afternoon of the fair, and because those silly Jylots disapproved of my Ballsaway game, I quickly made up a new version. The balls are black, the holes are black, but to make it a little less hard, I painted a face around each hole, which then became an open mouth. Kids love it, especially since the face is mine, as a clown."

"Naturally," Yobo said drily.

Ing frowned at his former employer. "So I pretended to be mad at Xeena when she demonstrated the new Ballsaway version and called the guard. How was I to know that the guard would snatch Xeena, stuff her into itself, and vanish down an underground passage, locking doors behind it? Garus, you and Xeena cooked this up . . ."

"We did not!" Garus pleadingly held his hands out to his royal relative. "You should have heard poor Xeena's screams—I ran to save her, but the guard had gone. Xeena's

78

been abducted. She's been stolen by this jealous, possessive court jester!"

"Poor little Helen of Troy," Yobo whispered to Jeff.

Luka stepped forward. "Your Queenness, I believe that Ing is innocent, and that Garus is guilty. It is true that Ing has made overtures to Xeena"—at this point Luka looked as if she were about to cry—"and naturally this has bothered Garus. I believe that Garus used his royal lineage to order the guard's removal of Xeena from Ing's presence. They have been quarreling constantly over which one is to sing with her. Perhaps Garus thinks Xeena is fond enough of him to consider the abduction a joke, or even a compliment."

"What's this about lineage?" asked Yobo. "How can that control the guard robots?"

"Orders to Izzian robots given by members of the royal family take precedence," said the queen. "Garus, what have you to say for yourself?"

"Luka's in love with Ing, just as I am admittedly in love with Xeena, so Luka's theories don't count."

"By that reasoning," said the queen, "neither do your theories about Ing."

"Stalemate, mother?" The crown princess's voice, Jeff found when he looked in that direction, issued from the holov monitor. "Cousin Garus is more than a bit conceited, but then, he's handsome, and the only one of us with genuine stage talent. I suppose everything he says could be acting, but you've known him since he was born, Mother . . ."

"Princess!" Ing shouted, "it's a plot to keep me from the final show of the fair! Garus wants to hog the stage . . ."

"Silence!" roared the queen. "I have come to a decision. If Ing has found a way to control the robots, he must be incarcerated until the guards are examined. Officer Luka, put Ing in jail—now!"

"But—your Izzness . . ."

"Obey, and return here at once!"

A tear spilled out of Luka's eye, but she took hold of Ing's arm and pushed him toward the door. With a haughty sniff, Ing said, "I am innocent. Yobo, you're behind this somehow, and I won't forget it."

When the throne-room door closed after Ing and Luka, Queen Tizz pointed at Garus. "I won't have the Royal Toy and Game Fair ruined by either you or Ing. I'm putting you on probation, for your innocence is not established. You will now return to the fair and perform well, doing honor to the fair and to our family."

"Yes, ma'am," Garus said humbly. Jeff thought it was a good act, until Garus looked up at the queen, his face pale. "Cousin, when the fair ends tonight I will find my Xeena, and prove to you that everything is Ing's fault. I am not responsible for causing those humiliating distortions to your image on holov. Surely you know me and my father well enough to believe that we would never do such a thing."

"I'd like to believe you. It is hard to imagine that either you or Orran would try to wrest the rulership of Izz from me by such methods, or by causing the economic depression that's turning the country against me. Now you'd best hurry."

When Garus had gone, the queen nodded to Jeff, Yobo, and Blawf. "I'm sorry you are visiting Izzcapital during troubles."

"And where's Pera?" Rinda asked. "I'm annoyed that you didn't bring her back with you from the fair."

"We've been to many more places than the fair," Jeff said, launching into a full account of the day's adventures. When he finished, the queen rose and walked to the terrace doors, looking out into the famous Courtyard of Guilt.

"You off-worlders bring me unsettling news. I have never heard of this key you say the Others provided to the ruler. As far as I know, neither my mother nor my grandmother ever had need of using such a thing, and it was never mentioned to me if they did know of it. I wish they had told me, for I need the key now, and if Ing has taken it to control this second Mainbrain I didn't know existed, then Izz will be taken over."

The queen paused, a smile erasing some of the fatigue from her face. "But I've put Ing in jail, haven't I! I'd like to see him do any dirty work from there."

"Is there a computer outlet in the jail?" Jeff asked.

"No. Not even a holov screen, although prisoners can watch one through the forcefield. Luka has undoubtedly turned it on so Ing can see the end of the fair."

"Jeff," said Yobo, "hurry to the jail and make sure Luka hasn't succumbed to Ing's persuasion. If he has the key on him and she let's him play with the holov outlet—it's connected to the main computer system, isn't it?"

"Yes," Rinda said. "Hurry, Jeff."

Jeff raced to the door, opened it, and promptly collided with Officer Luka. Eight huge guard robots loomed behind her. Jeff backed into the throne room, hoping someone had a gun.

"Here we are, Your Queenness," Luka said.

"Indeed. Taking over?" The queen went back to the throne and sat firmly upon it.

"Taking over what?"

"Wait, ma'am," Yobo said, striding up to Luka. Tall as she was, he towered over her. The guards remained impassively standing just inside the door. "Luka, is Ing in jail?"

"Of course he is. I always obey orders."

"And why are you accompanied by these guards?"

"Because, foolish off-worlder, the queen said she wanted to examine the guards. Here they are, all of them but two."

"And where are the two?" asked the queen.

Luka blushed. "I don't know, your Izzness. I sent an electronic command to all the big guards to wait for me outside the throne room, but only eight were there when I came back from putting Ing in jail."

"Without access to the holov?"

81

"The holov?" Luka blinked. "I offered it to him but he refused, saying he didn't want to watch Garus mess up the last performance of the fair. I left him securely behind the force-field, sitting on the cot."

"Guards, come forward," the queen commanded. They plodded to a line in front of her. "Open up, one at a time, beginning with you on the right."

The cylindrical body of each guard opened in turn, and the first seven were empty. The eighth contained a small robot whose round bulge of a head showed three eyes on the front and three on the back.

"Pera, my Pera!" Rinda cried from the holov screen. "What happened to you? We've all been worried."

Pera's extensible arms and legs came out of her body and she jumped from the guard. "I apologize for any inconvenience I have put you to. My internal clock tells me that many hours have passed since the guard snatched me. I must have been in stasis, for I remember nothing. I was trying to find out who was causing the holov malfunction."

"We think it's Ing, but we can't prove it so far."

"That is too bad, Princess. Jeff Wells, Admiral Yobo, and—I have never seen a live Jylot."

"This is Blawf," said Jeff, "leader of the Jylot. A guard robot snatched Norby, and another took Xeena. Those two robots are missing. We believe that Ing has a long-lost key that controls the Izzian computer system. We think that he has already implanted a program in one of *two* Mainbrains and that this program will activate tomorrow, naming him as rightful ruler of Izz instead of affirming the queen."

"That is terrible. What can be done?"

Luka seemed bewildered. "Ing's in jail. How can he do anything bad now?"

"You don't understand," Yobo said gently. "Ing's already done it. Just as the computer system has been malfunctioning for some time, humiliating the royal family and causing an economic crisis, so there is also a hidden program that on

Affirmation Day is scheduled to dethrone the queen. Unless we find the key or make Ing use it, we can't stop this."

"We could if we can find the missing guards, and Norby," Jeff said. "Norby might be able to find a way into the computer program."

"But he said he couldn't without the key," Blawf said.

"I think he could eventually, and I also think that's why he was kidnapped. Ing doesn't want him messing up the plans for the takeover tomorrow."

"You're probably right, Jeff," said Yobo. "The question is, what can we do now to find the other two guards, Norby, and a way to kill the Trojan horse?"

Yobo then had to explain to the queen his Trojan-horse theory about the computer program. The queen nodded gravely.

"I wish I had abdicated the throne years ago and set up a republic of Izz, but the people never seemed ready for that."

"Try parliamentary democracy, mother," said Rinda. "I've been reading about it in books Jeff gave me. You could still be queen, helping out and being the focus for governmental cooperation, but an elected Izzcouncil would run the planet."

"Except for the Jylot," said Blawf. "We run ourselves."

"And always will," said the queen. "I am honored that you have helped my friends from the Federation, and saved the life of Jeff Wells."

Rinda's slightly spotty face bent into a frown and she looked as if she might leap out of the holov screen. "But here we are all talking about the future of Izz as if we had a choice. Can't we threaten Ing with the Pool of Plurf? Maybe that will make him give us the key."

"Not plurf!" said Luka. "That will ruin Ing's career for a month. He won't be able to perform . . ."

"Luka," said the queen, "you still don't think he's guilty, do you?"

"No, Your Queenness. But I will bring him here if you wish to threaten him with the Pool of Plurf."

"First, I'm going to consult with my dear Fizzy, who's feeling a bit better this afternoon. Luka, I order you to return to the fair and watch what Garus does. Return in an hour and then we'll see about Ing."

The queen waited until Luka and the guards left. Then the queen majestically inclined her head toward her visitors, and went out to the king's sickroom.

"Speaking of Garus, look at this, everybody," said Rinda. The holov screen shifted to show Izzhall, with Garus singing the same song. This time it seemed even more sinister.

"I mean to rule our Izz—as he the sky . . ."

Rinda's face returned. "Oh, bother. If the villain is Garus, I think Mother would be only too glad to let him rule Izz for a change. She's tired—after all, she's the only Izzian who works hard."

"Princess," Pera said sorrowfully, "when I was at the fair I heard people saying that your mother herself caused the holov distortions of her image, trying to create sympathy for herself so she'll be forgiven for causing economic problems."

"That's outrageous!" yelled Rinda. "I'm going over there and give everyone ickyspot!"

At that moment, Yobo picked up something from a corner table. "I see that someone has given the queen a Teenytrip game. I can't believe that the queen herself, unless she's lying about not having the key, would be able to program the computer system to feed subliminal messages to anyone who plays the Teenytrip game."

"Admiral," Rinda said severely, "even if my mother had that key you say exists, she wouldn't be able to use it. She knows very little about computers. I'm studying to be court scientist someday, so I know much more, but I'm not the villain, because I've been laid up with ickyspot."

84

Jeff took the game from Yobo. "If you don't mind, Admiral, it's best if you don't keep this game. You might be tempted to use it and be brainwashed again."

"Nonsense, Cadet!" Yobo pulled on his moustache. "Hmm. Perhaps it's not nonsense. I won't play it. And I order you not to, also, unless you play it in the ship, where the Mainbrain can't get at you with instructions to wait for and welcome change."

"I know I'm only a technologically ignorant native—I mean, well, you know what I mean," said Blawf. "But is it possible that although Ing turned on Mainbrain Two because he found the key, he is not now controlling it? Perhaps Mainbrain Two was out of use for so long that it is malfunctioning. Perhaps the computer itself is trying to become ruler of Izz."

"Norby said the Mainbrains aren't conscious, but they are very powerful," Jeff said. "Perhaps consciousness develops if an artificial brain is powerful enough."

Yobo sat down at the foot of the throne and groaned. "This has been a long, hard day, and I have the distinct impression that we're overloaded with choices of villains."

Norby was a threat to the villain, Jeff thought. If I can think of how, then perhaps I can think of what to do.

13.

The Game

When Luka returned to announce that the missing guards had not been found, the queen was still absent. The king called to say that she'd been so tired she'd taken a nap and would appear at suppertime.

"Isn't it suppertime now?" Yobo asked plaintively. "Teatime seems long ago, although I suppose it wasn't. I'm tired too, of watching the blasted toy fair on holov. I must say that Garus is knocking himself out to make up for Ing's absence, yet people are still yelling for the court jester."

"Ing's popular," Jeff said moodily. He was playing with an idea in his head and didn't know how to put it into action without disobeying the admiral.

Pera had gone to Rinda, and Blawf was curled up in her own tentacles, fast asleep. Luka stomped over to the terrace doors and sat down, staring out at the Courtyard of Guilt as if wondering whether or not the queen would command her to dump Ing in the plurf. The throne room was a gloomy place.

Suddenly Jeff made up his mind. "Admiral, I'm going for a walk in the gardens. I miss Norby terribly . . ."

"Of course, Cadet. You want to be alone in your misery. I understand the feeling. I get it frequently at Space Command."

Jeff walked through the Courtyard of Guilt, giving the Pool of Plurf a wide berth, and out the back gate to the back gardens. They were beautiful, but that wasn't what he wanted. He discovered that his guess was correct—the princess's tower had a bottom entrance into the gardens, and he made for it.

"Rinda," he said, walking into her room, "I don't care if I get ickyspot. I need your help."

At the moment Rinda's spots competed with her freckles, and her red hair stuck out as if she'd been thrusting both hands through it, but when she smiled it warmed Jeff's heart. "Jeff, you know I'd do anything for you, but we in the royal family seem to be on our way out. What can I do?"

"I would like to help if I can," Pera added.

Jeff held up the game Yobo had found in the throne room. "I want to plug this Teenytrip game into the Izzian computer system and play it. Both of you must observe me carefully and if my mind seems to be captured—if I look drugged or I start babbling about change—you must pull me away."

"I heard everything you told Mother. I'm not sure you should play such a dangerous game. Didn't you say it took four naps for the effect on the admiral to wear off?"

"Yes, but it did wear off, because he only played it a short time. Your citizens have been playing this game for days, so it's possible the effects won't wear off them until well after the Affirmation ceremonies tomorrow. If the Mainbrain declares Ing to be the rightful ruler of Izz, then the citizens will probably rebel if your mother doesn't resign."

Pera said, "Is there any use in your taking the risk of playing the game if you might start to think like them?"

"I don't know. I think there may be." Jeff sat down in front of Rinda's computer terminal and inserted the Teenytrip game. He held the headband, surprised at how squeamish he felt about putting it on. "The second mode of this game simulates reality on a highly micro level. You seem to be playing with subatomic particles in a unified field, but I wonder . . ."

"Wonder what?" Rinda asked impatiently. "How Ing got the Mainbrain to insert that horse, or whatever you call it, into the game?"

"Trojan horse. Hidden instructions that have been per-suading people to expect, even demand, change. And worse, that have been causing random computer changes to under-mine the Izzian economy and turn everyone against your mother, whose holov image has been made to look crazy and evil. Ing used the long-lost key to change the Mainbrain. There's no mystery about that. I'm curious about the height-ened suggestibility promoted by the game."

"That's why you can't play it, Jeff. I couldn't bear it if you started to turn against the royal family—against *me*."

"But what if it loosens up my mind just enough so that I can be more telepathic? I'm usually not able to communicate telepathically with Norby unless I'm touching him, but sometimes I can under unusual circumstances when our minds seem to touch."

"Jeff, I'm sorry to say that I have been trying without success to reach Norby's mind," Pera said.

"So have I. All the way up the tower lift I concentrated, but I failed to get any hint of where he is, or even if he's still alive."

"You mean not deactivated," said Rinda.

"I didn't want to say that word."

The tears in Rinda's eyes matched those in his own, and little Pera blinked in an agitated manner. To hide his feelings, Jeff turned back to the computer monitor and quickly put on the headband that turned the game into a feely.

"Jeff," Pera said, "if Norby is still inside a guard robot, he's in stasis. I am unconscious in stasis. How will you be able to reach Norby if he is also unconscious?"

"When I went to a used robot store in Manhattan to buy Norby, he was in a stasis box. He told me later that although he couldn't move or speak in stasis, he could think. That means Norby's not unconscious in stasis. I am going to try to make contact with him, somehow."

"Through the Teenytrip game?" asked Rinda.

"While it's hooked to the computer system, which is controlled by Mainbrain Two . . ."

"Which Ing controls," Rinda said.

"Not at the moment, since he's in jail. He probably thinks his plans are safe because the Trojan horse program in Mainbrain Two is now running the Izzian computer system, and that probably controls the guard robots too."

"Probably?" Rinda shook her head. "Too many uncertainties, Jeff. You're going to try linking your mind to the booby-trapped computer system. It's too dangerous."

"I can't think of any other way out of this, short of taking Ing apart to find out where the key is. Ing's an expert at hiding the truth, and I'm not good at violence."

"I'll tell Mother to threaten Ing with plurf."

"He'll say no, she'll throw him in, and he still won't cooperate. Then what will your mother do?"

"I don't know. Beyond plurf, she's not good at violence either, and we Izzians don't have fancy drugs to coerce people into telling what they don't want to tell."

"Therefore, dearest Princess, I am going to play a game."

Jeff turned on the game's connection to the system and was instantly in another place, floating in an ocean that was not an ocean, space that was not space. Around him he could feel—not exactly see—that the ocean had tighter parts that must be what huge ungainly creatures like human beings called subatomic particles. The odd thing was that he still felt human but at the same time immeasurably small.

The tighter parts danced. They seemed so free, and although he was floating, he seemed to be bound. He wanted to be free, to join them. To experience change.

Change—the word pummeled his mind. He forced himself to recognize it for what it was—a subliminal message implanted in the game by Mainbrain Two's programming—but he could not get back to the joyful sense of play he'd had when he tried the Teenytrip game in the ship, uninfluenced by the Trojan horse.

Someone was shaking him.

"Jeff! You look so weird! Stop playing the game!"

He opened his eyes and turned around without taking off the headband. He forced himself to see through his own eyes and not through the machine. Rinda looked frightened.

"I'm all right, Rinda. I'm just having trouble bypassing the Trojan horse so I can use the game to enter the computer system and find out where Norby is."

"You're not all right. You look awful. Stop."

"I can't. I have to find Norby."

"Is the machine telling you to want change?"

"Yes, but I hope it's not affecting me because I know what game *it's* playing. But the Teenytrip itself—and blast Ing for giving it that idiotic name . . ."

"The better to conceal its true purpose," said Pera.

"Oh. Yes, You're right. Anyway, the Teenytrip is terribly interesting . . ."

Suddenly Rinda leaned forward, her lips pressing his. She clung to him, breathing softly against his cheek, until he put his hands to her head and pushed her back.

"You didn't like it? I was trying to be more interesting than the game."

Jeff laughed.

"Just because I'm not grown up yet you needn't laugh at my kissing you, Jeff Wells!"

"I'm not laughing at you, Rinda. Your kiss was terrific. More than terrific, because it brought me out of the clutches of the game completely. I think I can control it now. Be patient. I'm going to concentrate on Norby."

It was so hard. Once his eyes shut, the feely part of the Teenytrip game took over. Virtual reality seemed to become real, and he found himself sucked back into awful regret that he was not free like the—waves on the ocean? Particles in space? Nodes of probability in the ocean of uncertainty . . .

And then he knew why the game could force anyone to look for and accept whatever change the Mainbrain would dictate on Affirmation Day. The field of space-time-matter-energy or whatever his mind was inhabiting had resolved itself into one overwhelming impression of uncertainty that could be corrected only by the proper change . . .

He nearly tore off the headband, but he didn't want Rinda to know that his brave words had only been words.

Only. Jeff clung to that word. Only a game. Only a game. Not real. Not genuine reality.

He gritted his teeth and dug his fingernails into his thighs. The pain was real.

I'm a human being, on my own level of reality, certain of my existence . . .

But could anyone be certain of anything when the fundamentals of the field were dancing probabilities?

They flickered in his visual centers, vibrating, singing, out of his control—and he was in the field, part of it, lost in it, captured by it.

"It's engulfing me! Digesting me into the uncertainty!"

"Jeff!"

He grabbed her hand before she could tear off the headband. "Wait. I must not be so weak. I must—"

Jeff took a deep breath, forcing himself to smile. He focused on a picture in his memory, a small, shiny, mixed-up robot, and let the breath out slowly.

"This is a game," he said, speaking carefully. "I am tuned to the computer system and through it I can reach Norby."

Part of his solstice meditation came to him.

"We are all part of the Oneness. We are real because it is real. We are all connected . . ."

He let himself relax, focusing on that picture in his mind. "Norby—wake up! Norby!"

—Jeff?

The name flipped into his mind, not through his ears.

—Norby, you're in stasis, but you must stay awake!

—Okay, Jeff. It's very hard, but I'll try.

—Where are you?

—Inside the guard robot, you idiot.

—I know, but where is the guard?

—If I knew . . .

—No clues at all?

—There's something else . . . don't know . . . seems familiar but I can't tell . . .

—Norby, what is it?

—Big . . .

Jeff came to so suddenly he felt as if a plug had been pulled inside his head. He looked up to see that the monitor was dark. In fact, everything seemed dim.

"Something's happened to my eyes."

"No, Jeff," said Pera. "The electricity to the whole palace has been cut off. What have you done?"

14.

Ing

Jeff took off the Teenytrip headband, unplugged the game, and stuffed it into his tunic pocket, where it jangled against the gold point he'd taken from Ing's hat. He walked to the only light in the room, the tower window. From it he could see that the sun of Izz had set below the horizon, but the sky still had a glow that slowly faded as he watched.

"The rest of Izzcapital seems to have lights," said Pera. "The electrical blackout has affected only the palace."

"What happened?" Rinda asked. "Was it your doing, Jeff?"

"I suspect it is my fault, in a way. You see, I had just made contact with Norby. I think the power cutoff made sure I wouldn't be able to continue talking to him. Somebody must be monitoring the Teenytrip game."

Rinda put on her shoes by the light from the tower window and said, "The tower lift will be out, so I'm going to walk down the stairs. We must tell my mother. It's quite a hike to the rest of the palace—I hope you're up to it, Jeff. Here's a permalight for you. I've got Pera's built-in light."

"Rinda, I can't come with you. I want Pera to take me on her antigrav down the lift shaft to the underground passageways. I'm going to try to enter Mainbrain One's room and see if I can reach Norby through the Teenytrip game if it's plugged directly into the computer."

"You said Mainbrain One is only partially working, and anyway, it's halfway between the palace and Izzhall. The electricity to Mainbrain One may be out, too."

"Probably not. The Others were careful about having

everything fail-safe, so I'd guess that Mainbrain One and Two have their own backup generators. What I'm hoping is that the door to Mainbrain One's room is now unlocked. I don't need a fully operational computer, just one that will play a Teenytrip game. Goodbye, Rinda."

Rinda stamped her royal foot. "If you're going into the tunnels I'm going too . . ."

"No, Rinda. Pera can't carry both of us, and we'd have to walk there. I must hurry before the power comes back on. I hope you'll walk down as you planned, to tell the Queen where Pera and I have gone."

"But Jeff, I want to go with you . . ."

"No. It's dangerous. I have a plan—but it may bring trouble and I don't want you in danger. Do you by any chance have a stun gun you can lend me?"

Rinda stared at him for a few moments and then laughed. "My mother doesn't know I have one, but I do. I stole it from Officer Luka after things started to go bad in Izz."

"I need it, Rinda. Give it to me. Please."

"Only if you take me with you on this adventure you're plotting. I want to go along. You'll need help."

"I'll have Pera. You be my messenger to the queen." Jeff saw the stubbornness in her face and leaned over, kissing her. "Please, Rinda. I'm trying to save not just Norby, but all of Izz."

"Oh, all right." She reached behind the top books in a bookcase and handed him a small gun. "I'll be a good girl and walk down to the rest of the palace to tell Mother where you're going and why. Remember, Jeff, you're a Terran. Don't risk your life for our Izzian problem."

"It's my problem now that my robot has been captured. The villain may think Norby is just a pawn in the game, but he's more important than that, and I'm going to find him."

With the gun, Jeff descended the tower lift quickly by holding Pera's arms. Her antigrav took them to the sub-basement, where she shone her built-in light into a dark tunnel.

"This tunnel enters the main section of underground passageways," she said. "I know where the Mainbrain room is located, but I assure you, it's sealed."

"There's something I must do first. I didn't want to tell Rinda that we're going to the jail. It's under the palace, isn't it?"

"Yes. If the power is out there, Ing will have escaped!"

"That's what we have to find out."

Several tunnels later they came to a large, brightly lit room containing a few chairs, a desk, and a holov set. One wall of the room seemed open to what could only be the jail. Sitting on the narrow bed was Ing, humming to himself.

"Hey, Jeff! When the lights went out, Luka went to investigate before I had a chance to try out this song on her."

"The lights are not out here," said Jeff.

"Because Luka turned on the jail's emergency generator as soon as the palace electricity died, before I could escape. I was beginning to think the woman cared for me, but she has this regrettable devotion to duty. Now she's off seeing if security in the palace is still intact."

Jeff walked to the opening of the jail.

"Don't walk into it," said Pera.

Cautiously, Jeff held up one finger and touched the seemingly empty space of the opening. Instantly there was a spark and his finger hurt.

Ing chuckled. "If you must experiment, you'll get your just reward. Now listen and tell me if you think this will mollify our grim queen." He cleared his throat and sang.

"I beg forgiveness and mercy, Your Grace!
The games I promoted put egg on my face.
If the Ballsaway's fun was a bit overdone—
I needn't be sent from your court in disgrace."

Jeff cleared his own throat. "Ing . . ."

Ing shook his head. "Oh, well, I suppose it does need work. I'll adjust the scansion . . ."

"Ing! How do I get you out of here?"

"You mean you're going to spring me?"

"Help you escape."

Pera pulled Jeff back from the jail. "I must stop you, Jeff. I am an Izzian citizen and a member of the royal family and it is my duty to prevent the escape of a criminal . . ."

"No, Pera. The chances are good that he's not a criminal. I believe the electricity was cut off to the palace because I reached Norby through the Teenytrip game. Ing could not have done that, because he's been in jail."

"But perhaps Ing has put another of those Trojan horses into the computer system, one that is activated when someone gets into the system in a way that is dangerous to him."

"Oh, gosh." Jeff thought his bright idea had been dissolved, until he looked over at Ing, who was standing just inside the force-field, and had undoubtedly heard every word.

Ing's mouth was slightly open, his jaw down, and his eyes wide. He was either the universe's best actor or a genuine picture of astonishment.

"Trojan horses?" Ing said, his voice rising in a squeak. "As in mischievous mayhem, hacker hoaxes, and computer chicanery? Time bombs turning up in terminals?"

"That's right. A time bomb to be set off tomorrow."

Ing sucked on the end of his pigtail. "The fair's over today. Why would I put a surprise in the computer system when I'm not even going to be on holov tomorrow? It's that blasted waste of time, Affirmation Day."

Jeff made up his mind. "Pera, I'm going to take the chance that Ing is not the villain, because I find it difficult to believe that he altered the computer programming ahead of time to take care of strange emergencies like my reaching Norby. He couldn't have predicted that I'd do it. Even I couldn't. Some-

96

one else must have been monitoring the computer system and known that I was using a terminal in the palace."

"If I knew what you two were talking about, it would help," Ing said. "Luka will be back any minute. I'll ask her. She's a sensible woman, even if she's not a smash hit like our Xeena—say, has Xeena been found, or is Garus still hiding her somewhere for his own nefarious purposes?"

"Xeena is still missing. So is Norby, but I think I know where Norby is and I'm going to find him. You're going to help me, Ing. Pera, how do I shut off the force-field?"

"Jeff, I'm not certain that you should do this without Luka's, or the queen's, consent."

"Don't listen to that twerp of a robot," Ing said. "The switch is under the desk."

Jeff turned it off and Ing stepped out of the jail just as the tunnel lights came back on.

"I think I'll go find Luka," Ing said meditatively. "My humble honesty will convince her that I shouldn't have been incarcerated in the first place."

Jeff pointed the gun at Ing. "You're going with us. Pera, lead the way to Mainbrain One."

Ing peered into the tunnel toward which Pera was heading. "I suppose it might be interesting to see the Mainbrain—did I hear you say Mainbrain *One*? Are there others?"

"That's right, Ing. Come on."

"Fascinating. But I hear tell no one's been in to see any Mainbrain since Izz was settled. Must be dusty. I refuse to impair the beauty of my costume. One moment." Ing stripped off his flamboyant outer garment. The result was an Ing clothed in sleek black, as if he were a cat burglar ready for action.

Jeff almost sent Ing back into the jail, for now he could picture Ing skulking through the underworld of Izz like a demon, bent on mischief. Only Ing's black boots spoiled the image, for each was still circled by a thin band of gold at the top.

"Well, Jeff. I'm ready. Why are you looking at me as if I crawled out of a garbage dump? I'll have you know that this outfit has a remarkably stimulating effect on Izzian females, who, thanks to the fashions imposed by our dear queen, are not used to seeing well-shaped masculine legs in all their glory, unencumbered by baggy pants . . ."

"You've been playing Don Juan?"

"Just a little, Jeff, just a little. But I'm thinking of settling down. Xeena's too pretty, don't you agree? Settling down with her would mean endless suspicion and jealousy, for she's one of those females who doesn't know how beautiful she is, or what kind of effect she has on men."

"Like Helen of Troy?"

"What? Oh, certainly. I don't want to spend my mature years fighting off predatory males smitten by Xeena. I have enough trouble being fiendishly jealous of Luka's various suitors." Ing paused. "Yes, I admit it. I have become slightly besotted with our chief of police. Who would have thought that Ing the Incredible . . ."

Jeff shoved him toward the correct tunnel. "Shut up, Ing. Lead on, Pera."

Many dusty minutes later they found Mainbrain One's room.

"It's supposed to be sealed," Ing said. "It's locked, but not sealed."

"It couldn't be. Norby and I were inside a while ago and that's where the two guard robots found us. They entered by that unsealed door right in front of us. I'd bet that someone's been using the door for quite some time. Was it you, Ing?"

"*Moi?* You jest. Don't I have enough to do as court jester, holov manager, and Fair master of ceremonies?"

"You're also court scientist."

Ing's eyebrows raised. "I keep forgetting that. It's such a trivial position, since the Royal Science Laboratories are firmly in the clutches of ancient pedants who wouldn't know how to do anything practical if their lives depended on it. Furthermore, what can a court scientist do except design better games? Nobody can alter the programming of the main computer system of this boring country. Or it would be boring, if it weren't for me."

"Aren't you supposed to teach Xeena?"

Ing smirked. "I tried—at science she's stupid, and at softer endeavors she's unwilling. But she was willing enough to be in show biz with that revoltingly brash cousin of the queen's. Jeff Wells, do you honestly suspect me of kidnapping—what did you call her—I thought at the time it was singularly apt . . ."

"Helen of Troy."

"Hmm. That particular sweet Helen isn't going to make *me* immortal with a kiss, so as far as I'm concerned, she can stay among the missing."

"Ing, I brought you down here because if you're responsible for the Izzian mess, you might reveal something, and if you're not, you might help as a way of exonerating yourself. Now, do you have any bright scientific ideas about how we can get into that computer room? Something an intelligent court scientist might know?"

Ing stared at him. "If you're insinuating that I carry lock picks around with me, I don't." He bent over to study the door lock. "Funny hole. Got a pin or something?"

Jeff reached into his tunic pocket and handed Ing the gold point from the court jester's helmet.

"This looks familiar."

"It's the point of your helmet."

"Which that vicious Jylot stole and gave to you. I thought at the time you Feds had freaked out, but you must have thought you could use the point to get in here. Well, stand back. This takes a master."

Ing inserted the gold point into the lock and fiddled until he was red in the face and breathing heavily. "Strange. It worked on Luka's door . . ."

"Then it is a lock pick."

"Um. Ah, sort of. Part of Don Juan's toolbox."

"Perhaps you used it to open other things around the palace. Did you by any chance open something that contained another gold object with a point?"

"You're looking for something like that?"

"Come on, Ing. Did you find it?"

"I assure you that if I had, I wouldn't give it to you. I give gifts only to appreciative people. When, thanks to this magic wand of mine, I opened an old cupboard in the palace and removed some antique jewelry . . ."

"You stole some antique jewelry."

"Recycled, my Terran friend. I offered it to Xeena, who looked over her shoulder to see if Garus was around, which he was, so she said no, thanks, she has her own jewelry, and then I gave it to Luka, who thinks I bought it for her in an antique store." Ing stroked the helmet's gold point. "I'll have this put on a new helmet."

"Ing, try the lock again."

"My pick doesn't work, dummy! For this lock it's not the proper tool. See that hole—"

"I see it. The door, like the Mainbrain itself, requires a special key to open it."

"Then it's not pickable by any highly skilled lock expert," Ing said. "Where's the key?"

"Pera," said Jeff, "search Ing for another pointed gold object."

"Hey, she tickles!" Giggling, Ing squirmed as Pera searched him thoroughly.

"He doesn't have it, Jeff."

"Of course I don't. Using gold points on my helmet is charming ornamentation, but secreting them on me or waving them in my court jester act would be too hokey. I gather that the key to the door looks something like this and that you can't find it?"

"Correct." Jeff leaned against the door, discouraged.

Pera touched the door and said, "My function is to perceive. My finger sensors tell me that since the door has been unsealed, only this strange lock holds it shut."

Ing squinted at the hole. "Gimme the gun."

"No!"

"Well then, use it yourself, on full stun."

"Stun force doesn't affect locks."

"This is an alien lock," Ing said solemnly. "Full stun might knock out the electronic gizmo that runs the lock, or from the computer to the lock. Or whatever. Try it, dummy."

Jeff tried it, but the door still wouldn't open.

"If you insist on getting in," Ing said, "there's a good, old-fashioned safe-opening technique. Explosive."

"Ing, we have no explosive."

"Sure we do. Put the gun on overload."

"That might blow up the whole tunnel."

"Probably not."

"None of us is going to stand here holding an overloaded stun gun against the lock."

"You have no criminal imagination," Ing said, removing the gold bands from his boots. He handed them to Jeff. "I'd do it for you, but you don't trust me. Loop the bands through the gun, and insert into the peculiar lock. See, I've put a little hook on one end so the band will catch in the lock."

"Okay. Take Pera into the tunnel and I'll join you." Jeff waited until they had vanished around a bend in the tunnel and then hooked the gun to the lock. Taking a deep breath, he switched the gun to overload and ran.

He hadn't quite made it around the bend when the explosion caught him.

15.

Helen of Troy

The force of the explosion hurled Jeff against the far wall of the tunnel, from which he bounced smack onto Ing, knocking the breath out of himself and the court jester.

"Are you hurt, Jeff?" Pera helped him to his feet.

Ing stood up alone, scowling at them. "No one asks me if I've been injured by flying missiles consisting of overgrown cadets who should have stayed in the Federation instead of coming to disturb the peace of Izz."

Jeff brushed past him, through the rubble and into the computer room. To his relief, Mainbrain One appeared undamaged. He took the Teenytrip out of his pocket and plugged it into the giant computer. He was about to put on the headband when Ing plucked at his sleeve.

"I can't believe this. You blew out the door so you could play a computer game? The palace electricity's back on—see, the tunnel's lighted—so if you're a game addict you could have stayed in the palace and plugged it in there."

"It doesn't matter about the electricity. I want to plug directly into this Mainbrain. If I have a lot of trouble, we've got to cut those cables up there."

"Why?"

"They lead to Mainbrain Two, which is controlling this computer right now."

"Even if cutting the cables was a good idea—which it probably isn't—just what can we cut them with? The gun has gone kaput, and I doubt if even Pera's strength could rip those cables. They look strong and shielded."

102

"We'll think of something, Ing. Now I'm going to try communing with this Teenytrip game."

"It's one of my better efforts. A superb virtual reality feely if I do say so myself."

"Which you do not intend to use for treason?"

"Treason!" Ing squinted at Jeff. "Just what do you mean by that, you miserable worm of a Wells . . ."

"Let him play the game, Ing," said Pera. "Jeff knows what he's doing."

Jeff fervently hoped so. He put on the headband and turned on the game.

He was a small object in a cloud of small objects, resisting change that was inevitable. At first it was pleasurable, not at all frightening. He decided he could play a game with these objects—were they molecules?—and he did, hoping that mastering the game would help him control the computer that was making this virtual reality for him.

He laughed to himself, for it seemed so easy. Silly old molecules, now dissolving into atoms and then subatomic particles—or was it he who was dissolving, becoming small enough to feel, see—be?—what?

—Norby, where are you?

Oscillating probabilities? Is that all there is? The rest of it just the funny names invented by scientists who want to believe they can understand the field?

The unified field? Unified Field Theory? Is this an exam question, Norby? Why don't you come back to help me so I can pass the exam? Why does anyone think that the space-time-matter-energy field is understandable?

—Norby, I think I'm either going to destroy this field or dissolve in it. There's such terrible uncertainty. I'm going to control it all, stop the change, master the universe, or is it the field? Where am I? What am I?

"Norby! Help me! Where are you!" He was shouting aloud.

He came back to the human dimension so suddenly that it

felt as if he'd dropped out of a stronger reality. His body seemed strangely unreal, and there was an odd creature standing next to him, holding a weird object.

"What's the matter with you, Jeff? My game isn't supposed to make someone look catatonic."

The odd creature was a human being, like himself. Ing, holding the headband he'd ripped off Jeff's head. The only reality that counted was the Mainbrain room, and the task Jeff had not yet completed.

"You seemed to be in dire straits," Ing said. "So I disconnected you. What's the idea of springing me from jail and exploding that door just so you could have the strangest fix I've ever seen? I assure you my simple little Teenytrip game is innocuous fun . . ."

Jeff closed his eyes and said, "Wait. Give me a moment to recover." What he really wanted was to meditate, even for a few seconds, but not a line of his solstice meditation would come to him. All he could think of was Norby. Finding Norby.

Pera said, "Someone's coming."

Through the jagged door opening strode two of the big container guard robots, one holding a gun.

"Oh-oh," said Ing. "Luka's sent the troops after me. It would have been better if I'd thrown myself on her mercy and brought her with us."

Ing isn't afraid, thought Jeff. Either the guards are in his power or he doesn't know what they're capable of doing.

"These guards are not operating normally," said Pera. "I will go to the queen to report."

The guard with the gun snatched Pera up as she ran past it. Pera tried to withdraw her arms and legs into her body but the guard was too strong, and kept hold of one arm.

The guard with the gun said in the same deep, grating voice, "Move back into the tunnel to Mainbrain Two. You three must be made unconscious and locked in there until tomorrow."

"What on earth, that is, on *Izz* do you mean?" asked Ing. "Where's Officer Luka? I demand to be taken back to my comfortable jail cell."

"You interfere. You must be punished." The guard waved the gun at Jeff. "Walk to the tunnel!"

—Norby!

"Hurry!" said the guard, dangling Pera like a broken toy.

Jeff could see Pera trying to escape by activating her antigrav, but it was not powerful enough to shake her loose from the guard's grip.

If only she had Norby's hyperdrive and could escape into hyperspace . . .

The other guard disappeared.

"What happened!" yelled Ing. "The second guard vanished and I know I didn't pull a magic trick. Where did it go?"

The guard with the gun seemed to be scanning the room, but kept the gun pointed at Jeff and Ing. Then it lifted Pera close to its chest and said, "Have you done this, robot?"

"I am not responsible for the disappearance of your partner, guard, and I would appreciate it if you would stop trying to yank my arm out of my body."

Suddenly the guard seemed to grunt in disgust, and threw Pera across the room. She landed with a crash, but when Jeff ran to pick her up she righted herself.

"I am intact, dear Jeff. Do not worry."

"I'm sorry I got you into this."

Ing snorted. "Be sorrier you got *me* into it, for I could be eating a quiet supper in jail right now."

"This is all probably one of your acts, Ing," Pera said, shaking a metal finger at the court jester. "You are no doubt controlling these guards. You are a very wicked human."

Jeff was about to tell Pera to stop scolding Ing when his peripheral vision caught a sudden new addition to the shadows on the ceiling, which was even higher than the cave for

Mainbrain Two. Willing himself not to look upward, Jeff moved closer to Ing.

"We've got to hold this guard's attention," Jeff whispered. "Act mad."

"What do you mean, act?" Ing shouted. "I am angry. And acting is my job, you blithering imbeciles. I am an *actor*. That's what I do. I admit I've had my wicked days, but applause is better than power. I'm not controlling anybody or anything, but I'd sure like to get my hands on whoever's writing the script for these ugly hulks."

"You're shouting, Ing," Jeff said, assuming the observation would infuriate him.

"Of course I'm shouting! My day has been ruined! I can't do my act tonight and Garus will get all the publicity around closing the fair. Furthermore I'm being told that I have to stay in a tunnel all night! This is a fine piscatorial kettle you've landed me in, Jeff Wells! Especially since I am a respectable Izzian now, the famous court jester . . ."

Surreptitiously, Jeff stepped backward, further from the remaining guard robot, and pulled Ing back to him just as the dark shape near the ceiling fell with a crash that reverberated in the room like a local thunderstorm.

"Great galaxy!" Ing was pale. "We could have been killed! What could have—why, it's the other guard robot!"

"It is burnt black and badly dented," said Pera. "I am pleased to see that it has crushed the head of the one that was holding the gun. These guard robots have small brains, all in the head so the body can be a portable jail. Both of these are deactivated now."

"That's a relief," said Ing. "I must say that although it was a crude way of putting complicated electronic equipment out of commission, it worked. But how?"

Jeff picked up the guard's gun and bent over the blackened metal heap. The container doors of both guards were slightly ajar. Jeff tapped on the burnt one. "Norby?"

"Get me out of here!" said a beloved voice. "I'm tired of

being trapped in this stasis container. Not that the stasis works at the moment, thanks to my ingenuity . . ."

Pera rushed to the burnt guard, pulling at the broken door with all her considerable strength. It sprang open and Norby jumped out. He immediately clasped Pera's hands in what Jeff realized was the robot equivalent of a kiss. Then Norby inspected his own body.

"I seem to be intact, thanks to my good timing."

"What good timing?" Ing said, "Considering that you could have killed us as well as the guard."

"But I didn't. You see, my hyperdrive doesn't work in stasis, so I had to go back in time, which deactivated that walking jail cell of a guard."

"How?" asked Ing.

Norby looked at Jeff. "What is this villain doing here, asking questions about my methods of escape?"

"He's not a villain," Jeff said. "As least I'm pretty sure he's not. He even helped me get in here."

Ing was hopping impatiently from one foot to another. "Thanks for the good review, Jeff, but is that robot of yours crazy? Does he really time-travel?"

"Yes, Ing."

"Comet tails! He's probably done something to the past that will change everything, just when I have some great new holov shows lined up . . ."

"I changed nothing, Ing. I went back to the moment when the planet was condensing from assorted planetismals swirling around the star that became the sun of Izz. It was a very nasty situation that didn't agree with the guard. After a few seconds of being damaged beyond repair, the guard deactivated. I moved up in time and here I am, Norby to the rescue."

"You successfully damaged the other guard," said Jeff. "Let's see what's inside it."

Pera pried open the other guard's damaged door. She jumped back when she saw what was inside.

"It's Xeena!" said Ing, touching her. "I think she's out cold. Doesn't look injured in any other way, though."

Some of Xeena's dark hair had come loose from its clasp, and her face was even more beautiful in repose.

"So this is where Garus hid her," said Ing. "How horribly claustrophobic for the poor child."

"Since the guard's container is a stasis box," said Pera, "Xeena must have been unconscious all along. She probably did not even know that there was a crash."

"I hope my descent upon the guard has not given Xeena a concussion," Norby said. "Stasis does offer some protection against injury."

Pera, of course, heard it first. "Footsteps outside."

Two people made their way through the demolished doorway into the Mainbrain room. Rinda stopped, her eyes wide as she caught sight of Xeena inside the guard's container, but Garus ran to lift Xeena out.

"Darling! What did they do to you?"

"It was Ing!" Xeena's words were faint, her chest heaving as she seemed to gasp for breath. "He did this . . ."

"She's fainted," Garus said. "You monsters!"

Rinda lifted a royal hand in a gesture reminiscent of the queen at her most dictatorial. "My mother must be informed, at once. Garus, carry Xeena to the throne room—*now*."

"Can't I just go back to jail?" Ing whined. "I assure you that I had nothing to do with this, Princess."

"We'll see about that. Pera and I will go first. Jeff, you follow me . . ."

"With all due respect, *Princess*," Jeff said carefully, "I should bring up the rear, with Norby and this gun."

"Very well. Onward."

"Just a second, Princess." Norby climbed inside the container from which Garus had lifted Xeena.

"What's Norby's problem?" Ing asked. "A back-to-the-metal-womb complex?"

Norby hopped out. "Interesting. I will walk with you, Jeff, but if anyone up ahead tries to run past Pera, I'll be after them on antigrav, faster than a speeding bullet . . ."

"Okay, super-robot," Jeff said. "I'm glad you're back. Now, all of you—off to see the queen. And remember I have a gun. No hanky-panky."

"And that means you, court jester," said Rinda.

16.

The Villain

"Your Majesty," Ing began.

"On Izz we use the term 'queenness,' " said King Fizzwell, who had insisted that he was enough over ickyspot to risk attending the queen. Fizzy looked a trifle peaked, but his presence seemed to comfort the queen, who held his hand and stared grimly at her erstwhile court jester.

Jeff was tired and hungry, but the scene had a dramatic beauty of its own. In the bright light of the throne room, the ruler of Izz, her consort, and their daughter presided over a meeting of the accused and his accusers. Outside the dark of evening was lit by glowing lanterns in the Courtyard of Guilt, where the Pool of Plurf waited.

Standing before the elevated thrones was Ing, trying to bluster his way out of trouble. Garus and Xeena stood on one side of him. Yobo loomed up at his back, in case he tried to get away, while Luka, Jeff, Pera, Blawf, and Norby waited on the other side. Norby touched Jeff for telepathic contact.

—I found locks *inside* both those guard robots, Jeff.

—I know, Norby.

—How could you possibly know?

—I've guessed what really happened. But first I want to see how this interrogation of Ing goes.

Ing rubbed his eyes and sighed. "I meant 'majesties,' referring to both of your royal personages . . ."

"Get on with it," said the queen.

"I am innocent. Completely innocent. Not of inventing— ah, that is, *introducing* Ballsaway and Teenytrip games to Izz. I certainly did that, to everyone's satisfaction . . ."

"You brainwashed my subjects so they would be amenable to revolution tomorrow on Affirmation Day."

"No, no. I don't want a revolution. I want to work for the present government. I mean, not the Izzian Council, but yourself, oh great queen . . ."

"You kidnapped Xeena," said Garus. "Look at her—she's still groggy from being in stasis all that time."

"More likely from Norby hitting her stasis container with that other robot," said Ing.

"The court doctor has examined Xeena," said the queen. "She does not have a concussion or skull fracture."

"Whatever," said Ing. "I didn't kidnap her. I admire her beauty, but preferably from a distance. I leave her to Garus, who undoubtedly did the kidnapping himself, hoping to incriminate me. That's the truth, Luka."

Jeff saw Officer Luka smile happily. She believed Ing.

Before anyone could stop him, Garus acted. He grabbed Ing's ankles, flipped him to the floor, and dragged him out of the glass doors to the courtyard.

"I'll teach you to humiliate the royal family, destroy the economy of Izz, and abduct the fairest flower in the queendom!"

There was a loud splash, and Garus returned to the throne room, dusting his hands. He had managed to throw Ing into the Pool of Plurf without getting splashed himself.

"Sorry, cousin," Garus said, not at all apologetically. "I couldn't wait for your royal decree on that villain. I had to punish Ing myself."

The queen caught Jeff's warning glance and immediately said, "Officer Luka, arrest Garus and put him in jail."

"You can't do that!" Garus shouted. "I have one last performance at the fair tonight!"

Xeena stepped forward and said, "Please, don't jail Garus. He has merely taken vengeance on my behalf. Since it was Ing who ordered the guard to capture me . . ."

"How do you know that?" asked the queen.

"When I was inside the stasis container I was awakened for a moment. Ing opened the door, looked in, laughed, and ordered the guard to close me up in my prison again. Now Ing has been punished, so please release Garus. He and I will give our final performance at the fair tonight. You can all watch it on holov here in the palace."

"Before anyone else leaves this room," Jeff said, "your queenness should give Norby a laser knife to cut cables which permit Mainbrain Two's secret programming to enter the Izzian computer system. If this is not done, then tomorrow when the council asks for the name of the rightful ruler, the answer will be the direct descendant of King Orz."

"That's Garus," Rinda exclaimed. "Oh, I didn't want him to be the villain."

"Nonsense," Garus said. "My father and I are the only living descendants of Orz, who was crowned King of Izz, but we descend through males. You, Tizz, descend through females from Orz's younger brother, his successor."

The queen was about to speak but Jeff interrupted. "I think Orz's first wife had a female child after their divorce, and from her there's a line of females, also the direct descendants of the original king. Is it so, Xeena?"

Everyone turned to stare at the girl whose beauty seemed as marvelous and as fateful as Helen of Troy's. She said nothing.

Jeff walked over to her and reached for the gold clasp in her hair, now neatly pinned up again. She drew back and Garus stepped in front of her, a fist up against Jeff's face.

"I don't know what you're implying, offworlder, but my girl Xeena is as pure and innocent . . . Hey!"

Blawf had sneaked behind them, her longest tentacles reaching for the gold clasp set with the rich green stone.

"Get it, Blawf!" yelled Jeff.

Xeena's hair sprang out around her head, and Blawf tossed the clasp to Jeff. He extracted its gold pin.

"This pointed gold object has faint patterns incised upon

it. It's a key given to the first ruler of Izz by the Others. With it, the ruler can control the Izzian computer system."

"It also fits into a lock inside each stasis container in the bodies of the guards," said Norby. "Anyone who has the key can turn off the stasis and control a guard from inside. I thought it was odd that one and only one guard robot spoke, and even used a gun on a human being. The reason was that it wasn't the guard doing it, but the human passenger inside—a true Trojan-horse situation."

"Xeena, you stand accused," said the Queen. "I believe you are guilty. Did you conspire with Ing or with Garus?"

"With no one," Xeena said proudly. "Everything was my idea, known only to me. I was inside the guard by my own orders, not by Ing's, and I made up that story about his looking in. I worked entirely alone, and I nearly succeeded in destroying your economy and your hold on the throne."

"But why did you do it? If I'd known of your royal ancestry, I would have welcomed you to the family."

"But would you have given me the throne?" asked Xeena. "I did not even know I was related to you until the grand-mother who raised me was dying two years ago. She was born to Orz's first wife after the divorce, and in her old age she grew bitter toward Orz for leaving the throne. She made me promise that I would try to become queen, and she gave me the key that her mother had taken from Orz."

"Why didn't your great-grandmother use the key?"

"Neither she nor my grandmother knew what it was for, only that it was an important heirloom of the royal family, who had long forgotten its purpose—to make the Izzian computer system obey the mental wishes of its owner. It was thanks to Garus that I discovered how to use it."

"Then Garus was in on the plot," said the Queen.

"No! I told you the truth. One day when I was visiting Garus's family on Wildpark, I found the hidden entrance to Mainbrain Two. It had a strange lock I tried to open with the pin from my hair clasp. The lock not only opened, but when

I found Mainbrain Two, I could turn it on and give it commands by using the pin. I didn't tell anyone. Garus never knew."

"Oh, Xeena!" Garus said mournfully.

"I'm sorry, Garus. I should have shared the secret with you. But I'd promised my grandmother."

"Your Queenness," Norby said, teetering forward in a semi-bow. "If I take the key I'll be able to adjust the programming of Mainbrain Two right now, and correct all the other malfunctions that have afflicted your computer system."

"You shall do so, in a moment."

"I guess it's the Pool of Plurf and exile for me, isn't it?" Xeena said, hanging her head.

Luka ran to the courtyard doors. "I won't have you sharing a smelly exile with my beloved and innocent Ing!" She dashed outside, gave Ing a kiss as he sat disconsolately dripping beside the pool, and jumped in.

Queen Tizzle's laugh started as a giggle, and quickly progressed to a hearty guffaw so contagious that soon the king joined in, followed by Yobo and Rinda.

"I think that Ing the Ingrate has met his match," said Yobo, wiping his eyes.

Still laughing, Queen Tizz walked over to the now-open doors, through which a most penetratingly putrid odor was entering the throne room. "Ing—I apologize for the fact that you were wrongfully suspected. You may continue as court jester as long as you wish."

She paused, and continued while holding her nose, "As soon as the plurf wears off."

"We want an all-expenses-paid honeymoon," Ing said. "We're getting married."

"Anything, my dear court jester."

Blawf waggled a tentacle. "We Jylot do not mind the odor of plurf. As Jylot leader, I decree that Ing and Luka may honeymoon on my island."

The queen firmly closed the doors to the Courtyard of

Guilt and returned to her throne. "Xeena, I should be terribly angry with you, not for threatening my position as queen but for endangering the social and economic fabric of our nation. I think that even if Norby corrects the computer, there will still be the problem that all the citizens have been stimulated to expect strong change."

"Xeena," Garus said, holding his hand out to her. "Don't insist on going through with this change. I don't want to be married to a ruler of Izz. Why would anyone want to rule Izz if she has the talent for show business?"

Xeena took his hand and looked at the queen.

Garus looked only at Xeena. "Let's go back to Izzhall to do the last show. Maybe the queen will put you on probation for it. If you have to be dunked in plurf afterwards, I'll join you, and Blawf can find us a Jylot island that doesn't have Ing and Luka on it."

Queen Tizz chuckled. "Go, do the show. Xeena, I give you to Garus's custody—on permanent probation, without benefit of plurf. Providing that Norby gives me that key immediately after he adjusts the Mainbrains."

"I love you, Xeena," Garus beseeched. "Will you try life with me?"

She nodded, everyone clapped, and without waiting for the queen's permission, Garus and Xeena ran out of the throne room.

"Touching," said Yobo. "But what about the thirst for change? Won't that cause difficulties?"

"Not if the Izzcouncil becomes the first Izzparliament," said Rinda. "Studying Earth history has taught me a great deal. I think it's time the council members did the hard work of running Izz, and let Mother have a needed rest."

"And while parliament is running the planet, your gracious majesty can still be queen, the royal focus of Izzian life," Yobo said. "This has worked well for many places in the past."

"A figurehead," said the queen.

"Much more," said Yobo. "You'll be expected to provide wisdom and expertise . . ."

"But not orders," said King Fizzy. "Think of it, m'dear. We'll be able to go to all the major functions without your worrying about the work you've left undone. For the first time in our lives, we'll have fun."

The queen tapped her chin. "And when the government is criticized, the Izzcouncil will have to take the blame. I think I'll enjoy that. Norby, go adjust the Mainbrains while my Federation guests join the royal family for supper."

"Yes, ma'am," said Norby. "Afterwards Pera and I will carry Ing and Luka to Blawf's island."

"Dip in the ocean on the way back," said Jeff. "I don't want any of the court jester staying on you."

17.

Vacation's End

The *Pride* lifted from Izz, shot through the traffic patterns with a speed that would have come to Officer Luka's attention if she'd been around, and soon left orbit to enter hyperspace. Norby's back eyes opened as if he were checking to see that his two passengers still had stable stomachs.

"By the way, Pera and I checked out ickyspot. According to the data banks here, the disease is identical to one that was common on Earth, and to which both of you have been immunized—chicken pox."

"Thanks, Norby, now Jeff and I can go back to Space Command without worrying." The admiral rubbed his bare upper lip. "I miss my moustache."

"You look better without it," said Norby.

"I admit that it was a handicap when I kissed the bride. Remarkable female, that Xeena. It was fine when the queen announced publicly that Xeena and Garus are both cousins of hers, but I can't say I approve of the way the Izzian justice of the peace pronounced them woman and husband."

"I liked the other wedding better," said Jeff, "even if we did have to watch it on holov. Blawf officiated nicely, and didn't even bother to stand upwind of Ing and Luka."

"I'll miss the Izzians," said Yobo. "Even the queen, who is certainly more relaxed now that Izz is a parliamentary democracy. She and I played Teenytrip together the last night. She thought of very inventive things to do with quarks."

Jeff smiled. "You know, Admiral, when I was playing the Teenytrip game I went so deep into the simulated reality of the micro-universe that it almost felt as if I might be able to change the real universe if I tried hard enough. You see, if everything is uncertain, if we're nothing but probability patterns that may or may not exist . . ."

"I exist," said Yobo, glaring at him. "Space Command exists. Change in the universe may be inevitable but . . ."

"Yes, Admiral," said Norby. "I think there should be changes at Space Command. Make it more democratic, with feedback from even the lowliest cadet."

"Not while I'm in charge!" roared Yobo. Then he paused. "Well, I'll think about it. In the meantime, remember that every cadet has to pass all his exams. You certainly won't, Jeff, if you keep worrying about unified fields instead of studying Unified Field Theory."

"Yes, sir."

"The only important thing about the universe is that it's busy growing intelligent beings who, at their best, develop knowledge, wisdom, and compassion."

"You've forgotten to mention the development of brilliant robots . . ."

"That will do, Cadet Robot."

"And Admiral, remember that human beings develop one more brilliant thing," said Jeff.

"Oh? Do tell me, Cadet."

"Why, entertainment!"

"Hurrah for the court jester!" said Norby.